"You're going to insist I dance, aren't you?"

Zac sounded grumpy.

"Uh-huh. Just like the rest of us, Doc. Come on. I want to try. It will be easy for you because you've probably line danced a hundred times before."

"Never blind," he assured her drily.

"First time for both of us, then." Abby couldn't explain why she was so excited when the music stopped and folks waited for the next tune from the little band on the stage. "Explain line dancing to me, please?"

"You've been watching." Zac shrugged. "And I heard your toes tapping. Line dancing is just people standing in lines, doing the same steps together. Follow everyone else and you'll get it."

"Not much help, are you?" She reached for his hand, thinking she'd guide him. Zac started laughing. "What?"

"No touching in line dancing, at least as we do it here. You'll just have to endure me stomping on your toes. When I do, remember that you're the one who insisted I do this."

Lois Richer loves traveling, swimming and quilting, but mostly she loves writing stories that show God's boundless love for His precious children. As she says, "His love never changes or gives up. It's always waiting for me. My stories feature imperfect characters learning that love doesn't mean attaining perfection. Love is about keeping on keeping on." You can contact Lois via email, loisricher@gmail.com, or on Facebook (loisricherauthor).

Visit the Author Profile page at Harlequin.com for more titles.

Home to Heal

Lois Richer

LOVE INSPIRED
INSPIRATIONAL ROMANCE

LOVE INSPIRED®

INSPIRATIONAL ROMANCE

Recycling programs
for this product may
not exist in your area.

ISBN-13: 978-1-335-55373-7

Home to Heal

Copyright © 2020 by Lois M. Richer

All rights reserved. No part of this book may be used or reproduced in any manner whatsoever without written permission except in the case of brief quotations embodied in critical articles and reviews.

This is a work of fiction. Names, characters, places and incidents are either the product of the author's imagination or are used fictitiously. Any resemblance to actual persons, living or dead, businesses, companies, events or locales is entirely coincidental.

This edition published by arrangement with Harlequin Books S.A.

For questions and comments about the quality of this book, please contact us at CustomerService@Harlequin.com.

Love Inspired
22 Adelaide St. West, 40th Floor
Toronto, Ontario M5H 4E3, Canada
www.Harlequin.com

Printed in U.S.A.

Now unto him that is able to do exceeding abundantly above all that we ask or think, according to the power that worketh in us.
—*Ephesians* 3:20

This book is dedicated to the selfless
missionaries at home and around the world
who serve by spreading God's love.
May God reward you richly.

Chapter One

"Daddy!"

"Daddy!"

The double echoes of his four-year-old daughters ringing through New York's JFK airport came as music to Zac Calhoun's ears. Though the bandages on his eyes prevented him from seeing his beloved girls, his heart sang with joy.

How could a mere three weeks of separation feel like a year?

One afternoon Zac had waved the twins off to a friend's sleepover. Less than an hour later, rebels had attacked his Mali mission compound, tossing explosive devices that blew apart buildings and filled the air with cinders and shrapnel. He'd watched with horror as friends and coworkers fell before his eyes until a blast directly in front of him had ripped apart the hospital. Oxygen tanks exploded, knocking him backward and directing fiery debris right at him, scorching his face and stabbing his eyes, blinding him with excruciating pain. Mercifully, something had struck his head, knocking him out. He'd woken in the hospital to learn that his life's work was gone and he was unable to see. Worst of all, he'd feared for his daughters' safety.

"Daddy, we missed you!" Chubby arms now encircled Zac's neck as two wiggling little girls jumped into his lap and dragged his head down for soft kisses against his cheek.

"I missed you, too, my darlings." Zac clutched them close, inhaling their sweet fragrance, reveling in the velvet brush of their lips against his skin. "Missed you so much. Are you all right, my sweethearts?"

"Of course we are, Daddy." That was Zoe, always direct. "Abby looked after us."

"Yeah, Abby looked after us." Never to be outdone by her twin, even if she only repeated her sister's words, Mia hugged him again. Then he felt her lean back, probably to study him. "Abby said your eyes got hurted, Daddy."

"Yes, they did. But they're getting better." At least that was Zac's hope. Though the pain was mostly gone, the horror lingered. He'd been serving God so why had He let this happen? He struggled to his feet, loath to release his precious twin cargo.

He finally set the girls down because he wanted

to meet the amazing woman who had taken in his daughters. In the hospital, Zac had heard numerous tales lauding Abigail Armstrong's reputation and the orphanage where she cared for displaced children as if they were her own.

But Abby had done so much more. Since Zac couldn't see to travel and feared leading the rebels to the twins, Abby had arranged travel documents for the girls. She hadn't, however, been able to sidestep a government order that the girls must travel directly to New York to meet their father and so she had arranged to bring them here herself. Zac wanted to be certain this lady heard his heartfelt gratitude for her unselfishness.

"Where is your Abby?"

"I'm here." The melodic voice was calm, quiet, with just a hint of amusement coloring it. "Abigail Armstrong. Pleased to meet you, Dr. Calhoun."

"It's nice to meet you, too. How can I ever thank you enough for taking care of my daughters?" Zac had the sense that this woman was tall, probably up to his shoulders. The hand that slid into his outstretched one felt soft yet strong as she gave him a firm, welcoming handshake. "I don't know if I'll ever be able to fully express my gratitude, Miss Armstrong."

"It's Mrs., but call me Abby, and there's no need to thank me." Funny how he missed the warmth of her hand when she withdrew it. "Hav-

ing the twins was a pleasure—girls, careful," she
said when one of the twins bumped into him.
"Are you all right, Doctor?"

"It's tough to get a grip on the whole balance
thing when I can't see. Sometimes I wobble," Zac
admitted, feeling awkward yet grateful for her
steadying touch on his arm. "And no, I'm not all
right. But I will be," he affirmed stoutly, unwilling to voice the gut-wrenching fear that he'd lost
his eyesight forever. "Especially now that I have
my girls back."

"John Lawannie had a difficult time getting
them to me, but he prevailed." The sympathy in
her voice forced his next question.

"How difficult?" Zac feared the answer.

"He was attacked before he collected the twins.
After he arrived at my home, he collapsed." She
sounded sad. "A friend of mine, a doctor, came
to examine him and arranged for his care." Her
voice dropped, probably so the twins wouldn't
hear. "I checked on John before we flew out. He
was in a coma. The prognosis isn't good. I'm so
sorry."

"Thank you for helping him." *John's hurt because of me, because I wouldn't leave the mission when he told me to.* "Did you know John
previously?"

"Oh, yes. As a police officer he'd visited my
orphanage in a search for a missing child." She

changed the subject. "The twins are delighted to be reunited with you, Dr. Calhoun."

"Call me Zac," he insisted.

"Okay." After a slight hesitation she added, "It would be nice to sit and get acquainted, Zac, but it took so long for us to get through security that I'm afraid our flight to Montana is now ready to board. We must go. Girls, pick up your backpacks."

Zac heard the sound of scurrying feet as his daughters obeyed. Clearly Abigail Armstrong was in control. Good that someone was because he certainly wasn't. He couldn't see an inch in front of him with these bandages.

Maybe I won't be able to see without them, either?

He pushed back the dark thoughts as Abby's words sunk in.

"Wait a minute. *Our* flight? Where's Arthur?" Zac twisted his head, trying to discern some sound to indicate that the emissary from the mission's society who'd funded his work and accompanied him to New York was standing nearby. "Arthur?" A lack of response and the inability to see why roused disquiet in him. "There was a man here…"

"Arthur Strong. Yes, I met him a moment ago. He received an urgent text while the girls were

hugging you. I said I'd tell you he had to leave."
Abigail didn't sound worried by that, but Zac was.

"Leave?" Zac swallowed. "But—?"

"Arthur found a seat on a flight back to Africa,
which is fantastic because he hopes to retrieve his
own family. They were in an accident the day he
left," Abby explained, adding in a soft, sad tone,
"Poor worried fellow."

"So *you're* coming with us to Montana?" Zac
asked, half bemused, half relieved.

"And to your ranch. I hope that's all right."
Abby sounded as if she feared he'd reject her
help. Fat chance.

"I can't imagine how this impacts your plans,
but we are very happy to have you. Do you know
Montana?" he asked curiously.

"Not at all. I've lived in Africa for many years.
Moving to America will be a good change for
me," Abby said without the slightest hesitation.
"I agreed to accompany you and the girls to your
family's ranch and see you settled in. Then I'll
figure out my future."

"Oh." Zac wasn't sure what to say. He was
grateful that someone would help them, but his
eyes would need rinsing soon…

"Don't worry." The sound of a smile was back
in her voice. "I'm a nurse, Dr. Calhoun. I can
manage your treatment."

"It's Zac," he repeated, and then nodded. "Thank you. Again."

"No problem. I've allowed a couple of months to get you all settled. By then I'm sure you'll be well and I'll get on with rebuilding my life." She paused, then her voice altered, became more urgent. "You may ask me all the questions you like later, Dr.—er, Zac. But we must board now or wait until tomorrow for the next direct flight. You do want to get home?"

Hanging Hearts Ranch hadn't been his home for many years and Zac didn't have his own home anymore. It had been destroyed. Returning to the ranch with his girls—that sounded pretty good right now.

"Let's go." He'd no sooner said it than her fingers curled into his elbow, guiding him with just a few words of instruction to the girls to walk in front, hand in hand.

Zac found the going easy thanks to Abby's quiet commentary as she accompanied him and the twins through check-in and then along the jetway. They were a few steps inside the aircraft when she stopped him by putting his hand on a chair arm.

"You can sit here," she said. "It's tucked in so no one will bump you. Mia will sit beside you. All right?"

"First class," he mused as he sank into the

wide, supple leather seat. "Missionaries don't usually travel first class."

"I felt you and your daughters required the extra room and a bit of luxury after traveling for so long," Abigail explained, though she didn't mention how she'd managed to acquire the prized seats. She directed the twins where to sit but they immediately objected.

"I wanna sit by Zoe," Mia insisted. "We're makin' pictures about the mission for Grandpa and Grandma."

Abby waited for Zac's agreement before settling the girls in their places across the aisle and repeating instructions she'd obviously given before. Finally she sat down next to Zac.

"It's snowing outside. In March," she added, surprise in her words.

"Happens sometimes," Zac assured her. "You don't remember the unpredictability of winter in North America?"

"I guess not. Seeing snow makes me feel chilly," Abby mused. He heard the zip of a garment. "I don't think it will delay our takeoff though. Are you warm enough?"

"I'd like my sweater—oh, no. I forgot my carry-on." Zac began unbuckling his seat belt. "I'll have to go back—"

"I brought it." Abby set his hand on the handle of his battered case. As he dug through it for his sweater she said, "I'll see if the girls would like their jackets."

She returned a few minutes later, seating herself quickly as other passengers began to board.

"First-class seats are expensive," he worried out loud, suddenly wishing he hadn't left all the travel arrangements to someone else. He couldn't afford—

"Don't worry," Abby reassured him. "Someone donated these for you and your daughters. Be at rest."

Be at rest? Zac almost laughed.

Burning ash and bits of shrapnel meant he couldn't see a thing now, and in fact might never regain his eyesight. He was returning to his adopted family, at their ranch, as a widower, with his ministry destroyed and no clue about what his future held. Worse, he hadn't kept his promise to Maria to make *their* mission, *their* dream, something to be envied and modeled around the world. He'd lost it all.

How could he possibly *be at rest?*

"You seem upset. Are you in pain?" Abby paused. Zac had a sense she was checking her watch. "I was told you wouldn't need the eye wash treatment for another hour, but given all the time changes, perhaps that was incorrect?"

"No, that sounds about right." With no way to tell time, he had to trust that Abby's instructions were correct. "No pain. I'm just restless, I guess," Zac added when she seemed to be waiting for a response. "Tell me about yourself. You lived in Africa for how long?"

"Since I was thirteen. Half my life." Abby sounded surprised by that. "My parents were missionaries."

"Thirteen. Tough age to be uprooted," Zac mused.

"Very," she admitted, though he heard a smile in her voice. "I was furious with them for about a week. Until I saw my first lion in the wild."

"Game changer." Zac chuckled. "What was your parents' ministry?"

"My dad was a doctor, like you. He's the reason I trained as a nurse." Her voice grew more introspective. "My mom was a physiotherapist, but her real love was children. I think she always hoped she'd have a bunch but—" Abby's shoulder brushed his, probably in a shrug. "It never happened. So she devoted herself to me and every needy kid she came across."

"I'm sorry if I've caused you to rehash sad memories," Zac said.

"They're not sad," Abby said, a smile in her tone. "I often remember Mom's laugh, a lot more since Mia and Zoe came to stay. They have the same from-the-belly kind of bubbling laugh that sweeps you right into whatever they're enjoying."

"Do you see your parents often?" As soon as he

asked, Zac knew it was a mistake. She stiffened. There was a pregnant pause, closely followed by a swift hiss of air. "I'm sorry—"

"Mom and Dad died three years ago." The words seemed to spill out of Abby. "It was a difficult time."

"I'm sure," he agreed, thinking that was an *understatement*. "Did you come back home then?"

"To the US? No," Abby said quickly. She must have shaken her head because a swath of silky hair brushed his neck, filling his nostrils with a light floral scent that made Zac think of mountain wildflowers and warm summer afternoons on the ranch.

"Why not?"

"Because Africa was my home," she said. "There was nothing and no one for me in America. Mom and Dad were only children. Their parents were gone before they left this country."

"I was told you run an orphanage." He liked talking to Abby. She didn't flirt with him or gush about the twins, both of which he'd endured after Maria died.

"Ran. It wasn't really an orphanage," Abby demurred. "Just a safe place for children to stay for a while. I loved being able to feed and clothe them, to help them find new perspectives, often after life-shattering experiences."

"Which mission supports your work?" Zac

asked. When there was no answer, he grimaced in self-reproach. "Sorry, that's nosy. Forget I asked."

"It's okay. I, um, wasn't supported by a mission." Abby's voice changed, seemed to harden as she added, "I—we—I guess people would say that my husband was my only supporter."

"Was?" Zac couldn't have stopped himself from asking if he'd wanted to and he didn't want to. His curiosity about this quiet, competent lady grew stronger with every minute, which was odd because curiosity about a woman hadn't occurred once in the two and a half years since Maria had passed away.

"Ken, my husband, died two years ago. He was a pilot. His plane crashed. Our son, Levi, died with him. I came out of it with just a few bruises." The words seemed to spurt out in short, staccato sentences in a flat, unemotional manner. Because she'd steeled herself against the pain?

"I'm so sorry, Abby." Zac reached out, found her arm and slid his hand down it to give her fingers a squeeze.

"Thank you. It's been difficult, but God's will prevails."

Meaning? Zac's curiosity about that statement consumed him until they were at cruising altitude. When the flight attendants offered a variety of beverages, he smiled at Mia's choice of pineapple juice and Zoe's slower decision to have mango. His daughters certainly were children of the tropics. A few minutes later their voices changed, grew excited.

"What's happened?" he asked Abby.

"Mia and Zoe just received the cutest drinks with tropical umbrellas," Abby told him, a smile in her voice. "They're pretending to be ladies at a tea party. You have very sweet children, Zac."

"Thank you." He wanted to ask if she had other children, but figured that if she had, she wouldn't have left them in Africa and come here alone. Zac wasn't sure why he was so certain Abby had been a great mother, he just knew that was the case.

Why didn't she have her orphanage anymore? He'd ask her later.

"Daddy, we look just like those pictures of Mommy!" Zoe's loud voice made most of the first-class passengers chuckle.

"The girls talk a lot about their mother," Abby said. "You've done a very good job of keeping her memory alive for them."

"I've done my best. There are so many things I don't want them to forget." Zac shrugged. "Maria was better than I am at recording the important stuff."

"Oh."

He felt Abby's sudden jerk and quickly asked, "What's wrong?" thinking his daughters must have spilled their drinks.

"Maria and Zac. Mia and Zoe. How clever." Abby chuckled to herself.

"That was Maria's doing. Once we found out we were having twins, she spent the last three months of her pregnancy whittling down appropriate names."

"I didn't mean to remind you…" Abby stopped.

"I'm always reminded of Maria. But it's not as painful as it was at first. You must know that," Zac said, thinking of her husband and son. "The sharpness of loss gradually recedes with time, though you'll always miss them."

"How did Maria die?" Abby added cream to his coffee at his request.

"Brain aneurism. It was very fast. No lingering goodbyes or chances to say all the things I thought of later." Zac half smiled as the memories cascaded. "But Maria knew how much I loved her, just as I know how much she loved me."

"How wonderful to have that to cling to," Abby said in a tone so soft Zac almost didn't hear.

He was about to remind her that she must have the same tender memories, but he checked the impulse. Abby had offered no details about her husband or her marriage. Zac knew not all couples were happy together…

He heard a soft sniff.

"Excuse me." The clang of her seat belt and a rush of cool air told him Abby had left her seat.

Puzzled, Zac savored his coffee, replaying the few words she'd shared. He couldn't find any clue in them as to exactly who Abby Armstrong was. All he knew was that she was an excellent caregiver for his daughters.

He needed to format some kind of plan for his future, generate possibilities, figure out what he should focus on first. He needed to establish a goal. That was the way Zac worked best.

But Abby's fragrance, the most haunting perfume he'd ever breathed, kept drawing his thoughts back to her, reminding him that all his hopes and dreams for his mission, for his life, were gone.

Abby peered at herself in the tiny mirror and dabbed at her eyes. How stupid to get so maudlin over the past. Except it wasn't the past that had caused that burst of emotion. It was Zac's tender words about loving Maria and she him that had touched a raw spot in her heart.

Oh, to be loved like that.

"Stop it," she ordered her reflection. "It's finished. Ken's gone. You're free to do what you will, when you want. Free to come and go as you please, free to find a home for yourself or take up jogging. Whatever. No one can take your freedom away from you again."

If the Son therefore shall make you free, ye shall be free indeed. John 8:36

Abby repeated the verse several times, letting the familiar words erase the sorrow and longing in her heart. She was in a new country, starting over. Once Zac and his daughters were settled on the family ranch she would leave. She'd spend time exploring this second chance God had given. Why waste thoughts on a past she couldn't change?

Except for Levi. She missed his toothy grin and infectious giggle. How her arms ached to hold her little son close, to nuzzle his neck and press kisses against his rounded belly. Why had Ken insisted on taking her and Levi flying that day? Because of their argument? Because she wouldn't obey him and get rid of the kids she took in? Because she wouldn't agree that he needed a newer, fancier airplane?

She'd often wondered if Ken had been trying to punish her by doing those acrobatic flying stunts and if that had caused the motor malfunction leading to the accident. Had Levi's death been her fault? The thought haunted Abby.

Yes, she was free. She was also alone.

Blocking out her sadness, Abby exhaled, straightened her shirt and swept a hand over her almost-black hair, smoothing it to give the orderly, confident look she needed to assuage her inner uncertainty. Then she stepped out of the tiny cubicle. The sound of a little girl weeping made her hurry to Mia and Zoe.

"What's wrong?" she asked after hugging Mia's tearful face against her shoulder.

"She pinched her finger in the seat belt," Zoe explained. "Daddy told her not to undo it but she disobeyed. That's why she got hurt."

"Oh, honey, I'm so sorry. Let me see." Abby glanced at Zac, knowing he must be frustrated at not being able to watch what was happening. He was so handsome. Her heart picked up speed and she had to refocus. "It's all right. It's just a tiny pinprick. I have a plaster in my purse." She retrieved it and returned.

"What's a plaster?" Zoe asked. "Oh, you mean a bandage."

"In the school I went to, our matron—principal," she quickly substituted, "called them plasters. Let's stick it on. There. All better?"

Mia spent a few seconds examining Abby's treatment before nodding.

"Daddy always kisses owies better," Zoe said.

"Does he?" Abby bent and brushed her lips against the child's bandaged finger. "Better now?"

"Uh-huh." Mia quickly added, "Thank you," after her father cleared his throat.

"You're welcome, sweetie." Abby spent a few

more minutes reassuring them that their grandparents would love the drawing they were creating before she took her seat again. "After they've
served lunch, I'd like to bathe your eyes," she told
Zac. "Will that suit?"

"Yes, thank you." He chuckled. *"Will that suit?*
You sound a bit like an English schoolmarm."

"Sorry." Zac's playful grin knocked Abby off-
kilter and she struggled to regain her business-
like composure. "I was just telling the twins that
my schooling took place at a very proper English
boarding school. I guess I picked up the English
idioms there."

Abby hadn't wanted to stare, but now she studied Zac more closely. His dark brown hair was cut
short, but not short enough to prevent one wavy
section from flopping down over his forehead almost to his eyebrows. He was tall, probably six
feet, and very lean, although some of that may
have to do with his recent ordeal.

"Tell me about your orphanage, Abby. Please?"

Because the trip would be long and because
she felt sorry for Zac, who didn't have the luxury of studying other travelers or reading a book
to pass the time, she agreed. She would weave a
story for him about the country she'd called home
for so many years. But she'd choose her words
very carefully because, despite his lack of vision,

she was beginning to realize that this doctor was keenly perceptive.

"I fell in love with Africa's animals first." Perhaps she could divert discussion from the orphanage and its beginning.

"I can well imagine. I'm sure my girls would love to hear you talk about them," Zac said with a fond smile directed toward the chattering girls. "But I'm more interested in how your orphanage started. What prompted you to do such a thing?"

"I was newly married. We lived in Botswana." Abby ensured her tone was neutral so she gave nothing away. "I told you my husband was a pilot? Well, I often felt lonely. When Ken was home he mostly did the shopping, but one day he was away and I was hungry for some fruit. So I went to the market."

How she'd loved the times when she could go to that market on her own. Chattering in her broken Setswana, feeling the sun on her face, choosing her favorite fruits and vegetables without criticism about their price or how the sellers always gouged their customers...

"Shopping days were freedom days," she murmured, suddenly homesick.

"Freedom days?" Zac's forehead pleated in a frown. "What do you mean?"

"Just that you could buy anything at the market," Abby substituted quickly in her breeziest tone. "Hats, a shawl, food, books. There was this one seller who sold the most amazing handmade baby clothes—"

Memories swamped her. Levi's first booties had come from that stall.

"I don't want to make you sad," Zac murmured.

"You haven't. Just remembering." She inhaled and started over. "Anyway, I was at the market when I spotted a little boy sitting by himself at the side of the road, crying. He'd fallen and, I believed, knocked himself unconscious for a while because he had a big bump on his head. He said his name was Abioye, which means son of royalty. He'd been hiding from what he called 'the bad men' for several days. He was dirty and scared and desperately hungry."

"Poor kid." Zac's empathy was so different from Ken's disgust when she'd told him the story.

"I cleaned up Abioye and bought him some food, which he devoured in seconds. Then I sat with him to wait. I naively thought his family would show up to fetch him. But the market shut down, people left and still no one came." She remembered feeling as if they were shunning her. "I asked tons of people, but no one would take the boy. They wouldn't explain, wouldn't even talk to me. I couldn't just leave him there alone, so I brought him home. He was the first one."

"You never found out about Abioye's family?"

Zac shifted so he was facing her. "Lost in the sickness that plagues Africa, perhaps?"

"Actually, his father appeared at our door almost a month later," she said, smiling at the memory of how that regal man had simply strolled into her yard one afternoon. "He'd sent Abioye to Botswana for safety, but the boy's bodyguards were killed along the way. Abioye was pursued and got lost." She sighed. "That father had been desperately searching for his son for so long. Their reunion was very moving. Such love."

Zac was silent for a moment. "So after Abioye, other kids started coming to you?"

"Sort of." Abby tried to condense the tale. "Afa, Abioye's father, was the head of an underground organization working to stop guerilla fighters and instigators from causing strife in several African countries." She licked her lips. "Afa was so delighted with Abioye's care that he asked if he could send other children who needed to escape their homes, had lost their parents or needed protection. I would keep the kids for a while and when it was safe Afa would send someone to get them. I agreed. It was my way to help the helpless."

"But that could have been dangerous." Zac frowned. "How involved was your husband?"

"Oh, he wasn't. Ken traveled constantly. It was up to me to care for the children," she quickly assured him, unwilling to confess just how strongly Ken had objected.

"Still, he couldn't have liked you being placed at risk." The doctor tilted his head as if waiting for her to respond.

"No," Abby admitted very quietly. "He did not." Ken's protests had been more about him being inconvenienced than her safety. "But I couldn't just sit there and do nothing. I had to help. Especially because they were kids."

"So then…?"

"I think perhaps I should change those dressings now," she said quickly. "I'm worried we might be traveling through some turbulence later."

"Oh?" Zac lifted his head. It felt as if he could see through those bandages straight into her mind. "I guess that's okay."

Abby didn't want to talk about Ken anymore. She would help Zac and his daughters to the best of her ability, but she was never again going to let any man get close to her heart. Ken had ruined her past, but no one would get the opportunity to ruin her future.

Chapter Two

In all the treatments Zac had received since his injury, he'd known only one other medic with the same soft, soothing touch as Abby's, and that woman had been a nurse for more than fifty years.

"You're good at your work," he said when she'd finished rinsing his eyes, applied the ointment and once more secured his eye coverings. "Thank you."

"You're an excellent patient, Zac. No yelling." He heard the amusement in her voice and the click of her case as she stored her supplies. "Now, I'm thinking it might be a good idea for each of us to sit with a child while the meal is served."

"I don't know what use I'll be." Zac shrugged off the helpless feelings that continually plagued him. "But you're the boss, Abby."

It turned out, however, that the twins preferred

to sit together and share the meals which someone had thoughtfully preordered especially for them. Mia liked the fruit chunks, Zoe snacked on the vegetables and both girls devoured their pasta in record time. When they'd munched their cookies and finished their milk, Zac reflected on how to counteract their increasing restlessness until Abby suggested the girls use the earpods she'd brought to listen to stories she'd already installed on her iPad.

"You're so organized," he complimented her when Abby was seated again. "I'm very glad you're here. I wouldn't have thought of that."

"I've looked after kids, remember?" He visualized her shrugging after that comment. "Now, I've revealed enough about myself."

Revealed? Zac frowned. Meaning she was hiding something?

"I want to hear about *your* background and this ranch we're going to," she said.

Since losing his sight, Zac had grown adept at hearing undercurrents. He figured Abby no longer wanted to talk about her work or her disapproving husband. He didn't press because there were other things he wanted to learn about this woman.

"What do you know about Montana, Abby?"

"It's cold. Colder than Africa," she quickly added.

"That's true." Zac chuckled as he mentally measured the intense African heat against lovely midsummer mountain breezes that kept Hanging Hearts Ranch in the temperate zone.

Wait till she went through a mountain winter.

Of course, Abby would be gone by then. The thought brought a wash of sadness.

"Talk, Doc," she ordered.

"Yes, ma'am." He thought a moment. "Here's the short story. Years ago my family was in a car accident. My parents didn't survive it. We three Calhoun boys were adopted by Bonnie and Ben Halston, ranchers who run a beautiful spread that extends to the edge of Glacier National Park. It's gorgeous land, picture-perfect and ideal for active boys to grow up on."

"So you're coming home to be a rancher?" Abby's curiosity was evident.

"Doubtful, though I've always treasured the Double H—that's short for Hanging Hearts Ranch," he explained. "We Calhoun brothers found our refuge there. We were deeply loved and cared for by the Halstons and encouraged to become the best we could be at anything we chose."

"But you didn't become a rancher?" she asked.

"I'm sure Bonnie and Ben would have loved that, but—" He hesitated, then decided to speak the truth. "I've wanted to be a doctor, like my birth dad was, since I was six years old," he answered honestly. "Even now, I can't comprehend doing anything else."

Hearing his own words, Zac suddenly realized that he might have to reconsider his career choice if he didn't regain his sight.

"The girls said your wife was a doctor, too." Abby's quiet prompt drew him out of his introspection.

"Yes. Maria and I met in medical school. We shared a dream to build a clinic in Africa that was so well-equipped we could meet a host of needs. Maria was our primary fundraiser." Zac felt the familiar tug of sadness at the loss of his wife and partner. "But to your point, even if I did want to stay on the Double H, what good is a rancher who can't see?"

"The doctor's prognosis didn't predict that." Abby sounded—what? Sorry for him?

The last thing Zac wanted was sympathy. But before he could reject it, Abby continued speaking.

"If that is the Lord's will, and I don't believe it is," she added gently, "there are still many things you could do."

"I'm not ready to go there yet." Zac gulped, petrified by the thought of never seeing his daughters' faces again, never watching them walk down the aisle in their wedding dresses, never seeing his grandchildren.

"No, of course not," she said soothingly, but that didn't stifle the horror he kept reliving.

"The attack—" He gulped, barely able to speak. "It was so senseless. An attack on the vulnerable in the most vicious way possible." He shook his head, unable to force out the images. "The twins were at a sleepover outside our compound, thank God. I was blinded, by debris from the explosions, I think. Seconds later another blast knocked me out. At the hospital, police told me John had taken the children to a safe place. You."

"I'm so sorry it happened," she whispered.

"They cost me my mission, but I can't, I won't, give up my sight to them," he said, back teeth clenched.

"Don't dwell there, Zac," Abby said firmly, a calm comfort in her voice. "Maybe instead you could remember the 'whatsoever' verse in Philippians. You know the one. Whatsoever things are true, honest, just, pure, lovely, of good report—think on those things."

"Good advice," Zac agreed, the knot inside him loosening just a bit, though he wasn't sure he would ever be able to forgive God for not intervening. "I can't decide our future right now, so we'll stay at the ranch, take some time to adjust. While the girls get comfortable and my eyes heal, we'll forget about the future for a while. You must, too, Abby," he insisted.

"Me?" She looked surprised that he'd included her.

"You. You haven't said much about it, but I know that leaving Africa after so many years of living there must be difficult. Probably not much of a vacation having to be a nurse to me and watch two spunky kids either, but the ranch is a great place for sorting things through." Zac let his mind play back to the last time he'd been at Hanging Hearts. "There are lots of places to stroll or hike. Or you can just lie back and watch the clouds float by."

"That sounds like fun. Is that what you used to do?" Abby was good at turning the focus back on him, he realized.

"Sometimes," he admitted with a grin. "Mostly when it was my turn to dry the dishes."

"Dishes?" Abby sounded surprised. "I thought you'd have chores like feeding horses or…something."

"Oh, we did. But Bonnie was big on us boys learning to manage for ourselves, too. One day a week each brother had to take a turn making a meal. My brother Drew was the best at that. And we always had to help with cleanup. All three of us were awful at cleaning." He laughed out loud at the memories. "It was fun growing up on Hanging Hearts Ranch."

"My boarding school was not like that." A wistful note wove through Abby's words.

Zac guessed she'd been lonely.

"What are your brothers like?" she wondered.

"Drew's the eldest. He and I were always big into math and science. Nerdy," he admitted with a shrug. "He's a financial analyst for companies who want his input before they invest. He moved from New York back to the ranch to marry his high school sweetheart, Mandy. She runs the Double H for my parents and Drew helps her out when he's not busy forecasting stock market trends. They have a daughter, Ella."

"You said there were three brothers," Abby murmured.

"Sam's the youngest. Not nerdy at all. People oriented. He's a journalist." Zac waited for her to catch on.

"Wait a minute! Sam Calhoun? Your brother is a foreign correspondent for the biggest news agency in the world?" Like everyone else who recognized Sam's name, Abby sounded awe-struck.

"Yeah, that's Sam. He finds the hottest, most dangerous conflict spot in the world and heads straight for it." Zac sighed. "He's making us all turn gray early with his antics, but I doubt he'll ever give it up."

"He's single?" was Abby's next question.

"Sam was engaged a few years ago until someone didn't care for his coverage of them and kidnapped his fiancée, Celia. She had an allergic attack and died in captivity." Zac paused, reminded of that sad time. "Since her death, Sam's blamed himself. He never lets anyone else get close now."

"So he keeps taking risky assignments to avoid love." It sounded as if Abby understood his brother. "I'm sure you must miss him."

"Yes, and so do our parents." Immediately he felt guilty for not having bridged the distance between his own kids and their grandparents more often.

"I think you and Sam must be a lot alike," Abby said thoughtfully.

"Not really." Surprised, Zac asked, "Why do you say that?"

"Because you both found women who captured your hearts, and when they died, Maria and Celia took your hearts with them." Abby's voice grew softer, reflective. "You and Sam bury yourselves in keeping their dreams alive."

"How could you come to that conclusion?" he asked, taken aback by her perception. "You didn't even know Sam's fiancée."

"Nor your Maria," she agreed. "But I'm pretty sure neither Maria nor Celia would have stayed with a man whose vision they didn't share. I also think it's true because of the dedication both of you have to your work."

"Celia was Sam's camera operator," Zac told her. "She shared his love of a good story."

"Just as Maria shared your dream of helping the ill and infirm, of making a place of healing for those in pain." He had a hunch she nodded when she said it. "You're blessed to have such a wonderful family." Again the note of melancholy filled her voice.

"I'm sure you had lots of friends in Africa." He hadn't known her long, but he was certain that Abigail Armstrong was the kind of woman who attracted supporters.

Her answer was a long time coming.

"Yes," Abby said very quietly. "I made many friends after Ken died." A moment later she excused herself to help Mia.

She'd made friends *after* her husband died? The mystery that was Abby intrigued Zac. He wanted to know more about her and a lot more about the man she'd married, the one who disapproved of her helping homeless, hurting kids.

"Everything okay?" he asked when she returned.

"Oh, yes. The girls are fine, though I think

they're tired. I tucked them under a blanket and Zoe drifted right off. Mia's on the verge of sleep, too." A smile warmed her voice. "They are so sweet. How do you think they'll handle ranch life?"

"Hopefully they'll adapt. I guess I never really thought a lot about how this move would affect my girls." He'd been so focused on getting them back and away from danger. Their safety had been paramount. "I guess that sounds pretty stupid."

"No, it doesn't. Of course you weren't thinking about that. Not then. But I've been thinking about it now." She paused, then said thoughtfully, "With the kids who came to stay with me, I noticed that it was often helpful for them to be involved in something that engaged their attention for at least part of the day. Something they could count on going back to the next day. Are there active children's groups nearby that the girls could join?"

"There's a lot *on* the ranch that they can do," he said with a chuckle. "Helping my mom plant her garden or feed the animals in her petting zoo, to name two. There's actually quite a bit more than that to interest them."

"Riding horses, too, I imagine," Abby added.

"They're too young for that," he said firmly.

"But—" When Abby stopped, Zac guessed she'd been about to object. Her next words sounded appeasing, as if she didn't want to upset him. "I'm sure there are plenty of things on the ranch, Zac. But I was referring more to activities in which they can engage with other children. I've found that no matter where they're from, kids playing together helps overcome language, physical, mental and emotional issues. It helps them heal."

"I'm sure you're right." He thought about it. "I don't know what activities there might be locally for kids. I've been away from the ranch and the nearby town of Sunshine for quite a while. But I can find out."

"Do that," Abby urged. "Even day care for a few hours a day would help them blend in with the locals and the community." She had run an orphanage. She knew kids. But…

"I don't want them away from the ranch or me for very long," Zac blurted. "Especially not closed up in some day care. They can invite friends out to the ranch to play."

"But…how are Mia and Zoe to meet these friends?" Abby wondered.

"At church probably." He shrugged. "Of course there's Drew's daughter, Ella. She's around the same age. They'll be fine with her."

"Maybe." Abby hesitated. She spoke again, but this time her voice betrayed her anxiety. "After the accident when your parents died, did you and your brothers move to the ranch immediately?"

"No. We were injured in July and spent several weeks in the hospital," he explained. "Why?"

"So you moved to Hanging Hearts Ranch in what—August? September?"

Zac couldn't tell where this was going.

"End of August, I think," he said, trying to recall. "Yeah, because school was starting."

"Then you and your brothers had a few weeks of being the new guys before you became part of the school group," she guessed.

"I suppose so." And then he understood the implications of her questions. "You're saying school and the kids in it helped us find our place, helped us fit in." Zac cocked his head to one side to think about it. "I guess you're right. But it's only March. Mia and Zoe won't be going to kindergarten for several months."

"That's why I don't think they should wait to find friends, Zac. They'll be terribly lonely if they spend the entire spring and summer without any children besides Ella and without new interests to pursue." Abby touched his arm as if she was trying to soften her words. "Eventually they'll want to invite someone over, or to go to the friend's house. But before that can happen they need to meet other kids."

"Meaning I need to make an effort to engage

them," he finished, and nodded. "I know. It's just—hard not to have them with me."

"I'm sure it is. You've been through great trauma. You missed them and now you feel like you've only just gotten them back. But they'll be right there to tuck in every night. Positive experiences with others will help them feel secure in their new home." Abby paused, sort of diffidently, as if she was too timid to say more.

"I don't think you're the type of person to shy away from speaking the hard stuff so you might as well tell me whatever else is on your mind," he mumbled, pretty sure he didn't want to hear it, whatever it was.

"Well, I'm curious," she murmured. He could feel her scrutiny right through his eye coverings. "What will *you* do? How will you fill your time? The doctors said it will be at least six weeks before your eye coverings can be removed."

Zac noticed she didn't say "until you can see again." Because she didn't believe he would?

"I don't know about my future. I haven't thought about that, either."

"Maybe you should." Her voice grew pensive. "You can't just twiddle your thumbs while you wait to see. That will only make time go slower."

"What do you suggest?" he demanded, slightly irritated. "I can hardly ranch or rope or escort groups on trail rides like Drew and my dad do."

"No, you can't," she agreed. "But maybe there's something else you can do. Maybe that's why God brought you here."

"God didn't bring me here," Zac snapped, irritated beyond measure that she thought the loss of his African mission could be God-directed. "A bunch of murdering men burned down my mission. Because of them my best friend is missing and maybe dead. Men blinded me and damaged my hands."

"Zac, I'm sorry. I—"

"The question isn't why God brought me here, Abby. The question is, where was God when it was all happening, when He could have reached out His hand, spoken a word or even thought about it, and those men wouldn't have been able to kill my patients?" Though instantly ashamed of his outburst, it felt good to finally voice the frustrations that had plagued him ever since that awful evening.

Abby's silence was deafening.

"Until I can figure out the point of all that suffering, I'm not going to worry too much about why I'm back." He crossed his arms over his chest. "Now I'm going to sleep."

"Do that," she whispered. "I'm going to pray."

"I hope you get an answer to your prayers, Abby. Because I sure haven't," he muttered, and then felt guilty for saying it aloud.

* * *

Abby kept a vigilant eye on all three of her charges for the rest of the journey to Montana. She wasn't upset by Zac's outburst. He'd been through a terrible ordeal and no doubt questioned everything now. She knew from personal experience how hard it was to understand God's ways.

For instance, why had God allowed her to marry Ken when He knew that her husband was nothing like the man he'd pretended to be? The question was an old one and Abby was no closer to an answer now than she had been when Ken was alive. Which was why she shied away from dwelling on the past.

She'd help the twins settle in, build friendships and make the ranch her temporary home. Though it wasn't part of her job, perhaps there was something she could do to help Zac, too, other than providing nursing care.

Show me how to help them, Father, she prayed silently. *Show me how they can find You in their new world.*

Abby fell so deep into her prayers that she drifted off. The flight attendant's announcement that they'd soon be landing roused her. After waking Mia and Zoe, she stored their packs and made sure their seat belts were fastened. Then she checked on Zac.

"Abby, I'm sorry I dumped all over you," he began.

"It's not a problem," she assured him. "Everyone has questions at some time or another. That's how we grow in faith."

"I'm not sure religion can cover all my questions," he said, only half in jest.

"I don't think it can, either, because I don't believe in religion." She smiled at his surprised expression as she secured her own seat belt. "To me, religion is a generic name used to cover different views. It's wishy-washy. I believe in faith. Faith in God is what I base my life on. Faith is why I can trust God even though many of my own questions remain unanswered."

"So you don't ever doubt." He frowned.

"Everyone doubts at some time or other."

Now that she knew Zac as more than simply a patient, Abby could let herself admire this very attractive man. She especially liked his eyes, which, when uncovered, were a rich dark brown. Abby could imagine them twinkling with light-heartedness as he played with his daughters.

"Hey? Is everything all right?" Zac's face displayed his concern.

"Sorry. I got lost in my thinking." She smiled before remembering he couldn't see it and would need words to reassure him. "Of course I have doubts. It's what you do with the doubts that tells you how much your faith is worth."

"I myself have said that to probably fifty people in the past," he admitted with a wry grin. "Never had it hit home so hard before."

"The thing is, as humans we're always in a hurry. But God doesn't deal with time as we do." Abby tried to relax as the plane banked slightly left. As usual, the motion brought back memories of the day she'd lost her son.

"'A day is as a thousand years and a thousand years is as a day,'" Zac quoted.

"Exactly," Abby agreed, releasing a tension-filled breath. "We try to see everything from our human perspective. We forget that God's perspective is far different."

"That doesn't offer any answers," he challenged.

"No, it doesn't," she agreed quietly. "I don't have any answers. But sometimes it helps simply to know that we don't have the whole picture—about anything," she added.

"Does that help *you*?" Zac's quiet question was almost inaudible over the roar of the engines.

"Yes. I'm learning to stop asking why things happen," Abby murmured. "That helps me deal with my life more effectively."

"Ignorance is bliss, huh?" His words burst out harshly. "Sorry, that doesn't work for me."

"It might have to, for a little while." She touched his hand, trying to convey her empathy. "God hasn't changed, Zac. He still loves you and the twins as much as He ever did. I think you'll need to hang on to that to help yourself and them as you make the ranch your new home."

She withdrew her hand quickly as a frisson of electricity passed between them. It wasn't anything romantic, she told herself. It was just that her heart ached for him and for the huge change in his life that had him doubting. Clearly his faith had been shaken. Given her own questions, she probably wasn't the right person to help him return to his core beliefs.

So why am I here, Lord? What am I supposed to do for this shattered family? I have no answers and it won't take Zac long to realize my "strong faith" is a sham.

Abby tightened her seat belt just before the plane touched down. Some little voice inside warned her that in the coming days she would need God more than she ever had.

Could she make a difference in Zac's world and that of his sweet daughters?

Could she manage alone in this new country?

Abby didn't have a choice. She had to manage whatever came along because she was on her own now. That's what she'd wanted.

Wasn't it?

Chapter Three

"Zac!" Drew's voice in the noisy baggage area of the Missoula airport drew Zac's attention to the left. He judged his brother to be about three feet away. "It's great to have you home, bro."

Zac had never known Drew to be especially hands-on, so he was a little surprised when his brother embraced him in a warm, welcoming hug. Marriage must have changed Drew a lot. Why not? Marriage to Maria had certainly changed Zac.

"Thanks. It's great to be here." Not exactly true. Coming to Montana was a necessity because Zac had nowhere else to go. "This is Abigail Armstrong. Call her Abby."

There was an odd pause before Drew spoke, his voice filled with—what? Surprise? Confusion? Zac couldn't quite discern his brother's reaction. He decided he'd ask about it later.

"Pleased to meet you, Abby." They probably shook hands before Drew said, "I doubt if you girls remember me. But I remember you. You're Zoe and you are Mia."

"How did you know?" Mia asked in surprise. "Everybody gets us mixed up."

"That's my little secret," Drew told her with a chuckle. "You two have grown since the last pictures your dad sent!"

"Daddy, you gotta 'duce us," a chirpy voice reminded him.

"Yes, I do. Folks, this sweet thing is Ella. My daughter," Drew said proudly. "Honey, this is my brother Zac, your uncle. This lady is Abby. And this is Zoe and Mia."

Ella's hi to Zac and Abby was perfunctory before she asked the twins, "Do you like to play Barbies?"

They quickly agreed and soon all three were merrily chatting about dolls.

"I thought maybe you'd fly into Kalispell but I guess the connections didn't work, huh?" Drew chuckled. "They never seem to work for me, either, when I have to go to New York. So, is this all of your luggage? I expected more."

"Whatever was left is supposedly being shipped." Relieved when Abby slid her hand under his arm, Zac realized how much he'd come to count on her guidance.

"If you'll wait out front while I get the car, then we can load people and suitcases all at once," Drew suggested. "That way you won't have to work your way across a crowded parking lot."

"Thanks for that." Zac heard the swishing sound of sliding doors. Then a gust of cool wind buffeted him. "Welcome to the Rockies, Abby," he said when he felt her shiver. "It will get warmer, I promise."

"I'm h-holding you to that," she said.

"Oh, it will. Before it gets colder." He chuckled at her groan.

"I forgot. Mandy, that's my wife," Drew explained to Abby, "sent a shawl for you and sweaters for the girls. Zac, put this on while I get the car."

Zac felt the welcome weight of a wool sweater land in his hands and figured it had been hand knit by his mother from the lambs she raised. With Abby's help, he slid his arms into the sleeves but brushed away her fingers to button the front himself.

"Thank you, but don't fuss with me. Get warm yourself," he ordered, feeling helpless, a bit useless and worried that everyone nearby was staring—a grown man being dressed by a woman. "Help the kids."

"Ella's got that covered," Abby said, a smile in

her voice. "And I put my shawl on first so we're all good. Right, girls?"

The three young ones took a time out from their happy chatter to agree. Zac figured he should feel relieved that Mia and Zoe had settled in with Ella so quickly. But he didn't. He felt awkward, and that irritated him.

"Be at rest, Zac. We're safely here. Your brother will get us to the ranch. The girls are fine. Everything is as it should be," Abby murmured for his ears alone.

Nothing is as it should be, he wanted to scream.

Abby said Drew had returned and led him outside. His brother loaded their baggage while the rest of them basked in the warmth of the car heater. Moments later they left the airport.

"How far is the ranch?" Abby asked from behind him. She'd refused to take the front seat, insisting she wanted to be near the girls.

"About an hour and a half," Drew said. "Sleep if you want. I know you've had a long journey."

"I'd rather look around. It's so beautiful here," she added, wonder filling her melodic voice. "I can't get over how green it is."

"I'm really sorry about your clinic, Zac. I know how much the place meant to you, especially since Maria died."

"Thanks." Zac marveled at the compassion in Drew's voice. Marriage had obviously mellowed his usually taciturn brother. "How are the parents doing since the fire?" He needed to change the subject. Fast.

"Much better. Friends have completely rebuilt the tack barn so at least they don't have to look at the ashes and remember. Both of them still have some skin grafting to get through, of course. But they face everything with the same gritty determination they've always had." Drew's voice softened. "Your homecoming will help. They'll be relieved to see you all. We've been worried since we heard of the attack."

"I'll be glad to see them, too." And then what would he do? Zac wondered. Sit on his rear and wait for his sight to return, if it ever did, while life went on for everyone else?

"Some folks at church wonder if you'd be willing to talk to them about your work in Africa and about ways they can help rebuild it," Drew said.

"I don't—"

"Not right away, of course. Whenever you feel ready to talk." His brother smiled. Zac could hear it in his next words. "Miss Partridge is your biggest promoter."

"Oh, man." Just what Zac needed—the former librarian, now retired, and the busiest body he'd ever known in his youth, with her nose already in his business.

"She's actually nothing like when we were

kids, Zac," Drew assured him. "She's more mellow, kindhearted."

"Uh-huh." Zac nodded while his brain said, *Maybe, but she'll still want to know every detail of what happened.* And he did *not* want to discuss that publicly.

"Feel free to nod off for a while, bro," Drew told him. "You've been traveling for hours and that flight from New York is worse than the redeye one. Trust me, I've done both enough times."

"Maybe I will." Zac had no intention of napping. He closed his eyes, but that was mostly to avoid further discussion about the mission. Maybe one day he'd be ready to rehash that day with his older brother, but not yet.

Actually, Zac did sleep, deeply and without dreams, only to awaken as they pulled in under the arched wrought iron gates that proclaimed this land Hanging Hearts Ranch.

"Welcome home, family," Drew said cheerfully.

Zac answered the twins' questions as fast as he could, but they came too quickly. He was relieved when Abby intervened. Did she realize how hard his head had begun to throb?

"Girls, I think Uncle Drew and Ella will probably take you on a little tour of the ranch later and tell you all you need to know," she chided. "You don't have to rush to learn it all at once."

"Abby's right. I will take you both for a good look-see around the place. But first we'll have some lunch," Drew said. "Ma's been cooking up a storm for days."

"I wish she hadn't gone to so much trouble. I'm sure the burns on her hands still bother her." Zac suddenly realized he'd become an enormous pain to everyone. "Plain sandwiches or canned soup would have been enough."

"You can't have forgotten our mother that quickly, bro." Drew laughed heartily as he parked, probably in front of the big house. "Suffering a little pain for one of her chicks is a sacrifice Ma will make every time. Don't worry. Mandy made sure she didn't overdo it. Now let's get inside so the parents can assure themselves you're all okay."

Zac had barely stepped out of the vehicle when he heard his mother shriek. A second later her arms enfolded him and held on.

"Oh, Zac, praise the Lord you're all right." Bonnie bathed his face in kisses where the cuts and bruises had healed enough not to be raw. "I'm so glad you're home, dear."

"Thanks, Mom. Glad to be here with you." Her embrace felt so good—safe, tender, loving. "Thank you for having us. Dad's here, too?"

"Right here, son," the bass voice boomed. "Ditto what your mother said."

Zac savored his father's gripping handshake and the familiar slap on the shoulder as he fought a tidal wave of emotion. His parents, at least, had not changed. Still offering comfort in a world that had turned upside down.

"This is Abigail Armstrong," he said, remembering his manners after the delighted grandparents had acquainted themselves with their grandchildren. "She took in Mia and Zoe and cared for them when I couldn't. She met me in New York with the girls and accompanied us all the way here. Abby's agreed to stay for a couple of months while we adjust."

Once again there was an odd pause. Zac couldn't figure out why.

"We're, uh, very glad to meet and welcome you, Miss Armstrong," his parents finally responded in unison.

"It's Mrs.," Zac corrected.

"Actually, it's Abby. It's lovely to meet you, Mr. and Mrs. Halston." It was the first time Zac had heard Abby hesitate. "I hope it won't be a problem if I stay until your son and the girls are settled in?"

"My dear, our home has been horribly empty since the boys left." Zac was pretty sure his mom had linked her arm with Abby's because Bonnie was a woman who liked to touch. Her voice dropped to a murmur he was meant to hear. "But to tell you the truth, the testosterone around here gets a bit overwhelming sometimes. It will be nice to have another female on the land. By the way, this is Drew's wife, Mandy."

"Hi, Abby. And hello to you, big brother." Mandy hugged Zac. "How goes it?" She'd never skirted around an issue she could face head-on.

"Pretty good for an old blind guy." Zac returned her hug. He'd known Mandy since he and his brothers had first arrived at Hanging Hearts Ranch because she'd lived next door. She was a true cowgirl, yet Zac had never known anyone more feminine. "How's married life with the perfectionist?"

"Drew is improving," Mandy said, not so quietly. "Slowly."

"Hey! It's hard to improve on perfection." Drew might pretend he was affronted, but Zac was pretty sure his brother enjoyed the repartee.

"Haven't cured him of his pride yet, I see," Zac teased.

"What are we standing outside for? Come on in, folks," Ben urged.

Grateful for Abby's surreptitious grip on his arm, Zac followed her murmured directions.

"Two steps up. Good. Through the door now." Her voice was so quiet no one seemed to notice as the others continued to laugh and jest on their way into the house. "Turning right here." When he would have gone too far, she gently tugged on his arm to stop him.

"Thanks. I guess I forgot where the doorway is," he muttered, embarrassed by his faux pas.

"Nobody noticed," she murmured. Apparently she was right because conversation continued until his mom intervened.

"I thought a fresh vegetable soup with some homemade rolls might be easiest for you to manage, son." Bonnie's voice felt like one of her quilts, snug and comforting. "Why don't you and Abby sit here?" There was the sound of a chair scraping against the floor. "The girls can sit at the little table and the rest of us will just gather around."

Thanks to Abby, Zac didn't trip or stumble while seating himself. He was relieved when she sank down beside him and quietly explained about the table settings, even though it emphasized how helpless he truly was. The banter was easy to follow but he didn't offer much himself, content to let it flow around him, their teasing a salve to his battered heart.

It was only when Mandy asked Abby about her family that Zac paid closer attention, noting that his nurse glossed over the fact that she was a widow and had no family. She also didn't mention that her son had died. And if Abby had made any concrete plans for her future, she kept them to herself.

"I'm not sure what I'll do when my job here is finished," she said thoughtfully. "Maybe I'll spend some time getting to know this country."

"That's a great idea." That was Ben, the enthusiast Zac remembered. "You're always welcome to come back to the Double H."

"Yes, please return as often as you can," Bonnie added. "We have folks coming and going all the time and we love it."

"Thank you." Abby shifted in her chair, her arm brushing his. "Perhaps after lunch you'll show me where Zac and the girls will be staying. I'd like to get them settled and unpacked."

"The log house you saw on the way in is where we'll stay. Right, Mom?" Zac waited for his mother to agree before facing Abby. "It's perfect. Not too big and I'm familiar with every nook and cranny. As kids, Drew, Sam and I used to play in there if no one was using it. Should be easy to find my way around."

"Would you mind staying with us, Abby? There's a large bedroom upstairs with its own bath, and Ben has rigged an intercom so that if the girls or Zac need you, you'll hear them call," Bonnie explained. "Will that work?"

"It sounds perfect," Abby said. "Thank you so much."

"Don't fill up on this soup," Bonnie said, the ladle tinkling against china. Zac figured she was serving her soup. "I made strawberry rhubarb pie for dessert."

"What's rhubarb?" Zoe sounded hesitant.

"It grows in Grandma's garden," Ella explained. "It's really sour if you eat it by itself. But Grandma adds strawberries and puts ice cream on top so it's yummy."

"You and Mia can try some and see if you like it," Bonnie offered.

"I haven't had rhubarb pie in eons." Zac's mouth watered. "Actually, I haven't had any pie in eons."

"Must be why you're so thin," Bonnie grumbled. "Some homegrown food will do you good."

"Fatten me up, you mean." Zac glanced in the direction he'd heard Drew's voice. "How much weight have you gained since you moved back home?"

"None. My wife works me too hard for me to gain an ounce." Drew chuckled at Mandy's protest. "She's always got another job for me."

"Does you good to get out from your numbers dreamworld once in a while, cowboy," Mandy shot back.

Zac bowed his head as his dad asked a blessing on the food, then cupped his hands around the big, warm bowl, content to savor this safe, happy place. Breathing in the aromas of his mom's cooking brought back so many memories. The girls chattered and giggled just as he and his brothers had done so long ago. It was almost as if—

Abby's soft fingers guided his hand to his spoon.

"I've buttered a roll. On a plate to your left," she whispered, her breath brushing his ear, her enticing fragrance somehow imparting a sense of calm.

"Thanks." Zac tasted the soup. There was no one depending on him here, no life and death situation, no disease requiring a cure that he needed to ponder. It felt like his soul could stop asking, *Why, God?* long enough to inhale and loosen up. It might take a while to let his vigilant guard down, though.

And then what? his brain demanded.

Zac had no answer to that.

Abby savored every second of the family meal, impacted by the love swirling around this table. Bonnie and Ben clearly adored one another, hands brushing each other's shoulders, eyes exchanging tender glances. Drew also found plenty of excuses to touch Mandy and his face lit up every time he glanced her way.

What was it like to be loved so much, so dearly, so completely? Once, Abby thought she'd known.

She'd thought she'd found that kind of love with Ken. But it was a mirage, a mask he wore until he learned how much money she had. Was that why Ken's about-face hurt so much? Because she'd been deceived and betrayed by someone who claimed to be a child of the same God she served, but who had turned into a greedy, grasping person who seemed to hate her more with each day that passed? A man who, once he'd seen her bank statement, once she'd refused to spend exorbitant amounts on toys he wanted, became a man she didn't know? Was his anger fueled by her refusals to give in when he threatened her? Had knowing she had more money than he made him feel inferior? The questions about Ken never ended.

Perhaps seeing the others so deeply in love hurt more because Abby had come to accept that she would never know that kind of love, never be cherished like Bonnie and Mandy were. Or perhaps it was because she'd finally realized she couldn't allow herself to be vulnerable again. Ken's abuse had wounded too deeply, taken too long to recover from, if she had yet recovered.

No, she'd never fall in love again. But making that decision meant she was depriving herself of the opportunity to enjoy what Bonnie and Mandy had. Abby had never realized how utterly costly that decision would be. But what else was she to do? She could not revert to that scared, silly shadow of herself ever again.

"Hey, did you fall asleep?" Zac's elbow nudged her side.

Suddenly aware that everyone was staring at her, Abby's cheeks burned with embarrassment.

"Sorry. I got lost in admiring your happy family," she said quickly, hoping that excused her lack of attention. "It's so wonderful to see."

"I'm sorry you have no family of your own, Abby, but I'm thrilled you're here with us." Bonnie's eyes softened. "Family is one of God's biggest blessings."

"Yep," Ben agreed with his wife. "The world looks a lot less scary when you know where you belong."

Where do I belong? Abby wondered.

"You c'n 'dopt our fam'ly," Ella said brightly. "Then Mia and Zoe c'n be my cousins."

"They already are, sweetheart." Drew grinned at his daughter, his love for her apparent. "But sharing our family is a great idea. So welcome to the family, Abby."

"Oh. Thank you. But I wasn't hinting—" she hurried to explain, but Zac cut her off.

"They know you weren't." He chuckled. "It's just that adopting folks is what this family does."

"I'm one of their adoptees, too," Mandy said cheerfully. "And speaking of adopting, Miss Partridge stopped by early this morning for her usual riding lesson. She was asking about you, Zac— said she'd like to speak to you privately when you have a free moment."

"I'm at a loss to understand how the lady's riding lesson relates to your comment about adoption, but I'd like a chance to get settled before I start seeing anyone," Zac said quickly. "Maybe she can visit in a couple of days."

Though she hadn't known the former missionary long, Abby felt Zac was trying to avoid meeting with this Miss Partridge. She couldn't help but wonder why.

Ella began telling knock-knock jokes and the atmosphere lightened considerably. When they had finished their meal, including Bonnie's sumptuous pie, everyone sat around talking until Abby noticed Zac drooping. Poor man; he was worn out. She rose.

"That was so delicious, Bonnie. Thank you. I'll help with cleanup." She began collecting dishes until Mandy stopped her.

"Drew and I will load the dishwasher," she said. "Bonnie wants to show you your room. I'm sure you'd like to get settled in."

"I would, thank you. But I'd rather we get Zac and the girls settled first, if that's okay?" Abby saw surprise fill Bonnie and Ben's faces, as if they hadn't expected her to take charge so soon.

"Of course," Bonnie murmured as she rose. "I keep forgetting how far you've all traveled."

"If Dad will help Mandy clean up, I'll get your luggage into the house, Zac." Drew turned away, then stopped. "Do you want a ride to the log cabin?"

"No, thanks. We'll walk over." Zac snickered. "I know you're trying to find a way out of dishes. You always did."

"You should talk," Drew snorted. "As I recall, you disappeared after every meal. Come on, Ella, girls. You can help carry stuff."

"I'll help, too," Bonnie declared.

"Mom, your burns—" Zac stopped short, obviously wondering how much he should refer to the fire and their injuries from it.

"Are healing," Bonnie said firmly. "I'll wear my gloves. They'll protect my skin."

"Let's go," Zac muttered to Abby.

He seemed in a hurry and she wasn't certain why, until they were walking toward his new home.

"What did Mom's hands look like?" he asked very quietly.

"You can see places where they've grafted, but they look to be healing well," Abby told him.

"I can hear her catching up to us," he whispered. "Make sure she doesn't lift anything heavy, will you?"

"Of course." Abby liked this protective side of Zac. Liked it a lot. It spoke volumes about the kind of man he was. But then he stumbled and she reminded herself to keep her focus on her job and off the handsome doctor.

"We had the place cleaned from top to bottom," Bonnie said, now walking beside them. "I don't remember how things were arranged when you were last here—what? Four years ago?"

"That long?" Zac frowned, then nodded. "Maybe it was. The girls were babies, I remember."

"Anyway, it's a little less cluttered so it should be easy for you to find your way around, honey." Bonnie studied her son, concern darkening her eyes.

"It's great. Thanks, Mom." Zac stopped and lifted his head when Abby told him they were at the bottom of the steps. "Can you give me the lay of the land? I need to orient myself, mentally organize what's changed around here."

"Sure." Bonnie described the open area to the left where Zac remembered climbing a tree and falling, breaking his wrist. "There's a playset there now."

"Beyond that is a paddock, I think. Beside it is a ring for Mandy to teach her riding classes, if I remember from your emails." Zac nodded, then said to Abby, "Mom used to teach there, too. I don't know if she still does."

"Occasionally," Bonnie said with a smile. "Behind that is Peace Meadow, where your youth group used to play Capture the Flag. We've pretty much left it as is. Of course, the barns are still in the same place, though most of our animals stay out now that it's getting warmer."

"Your petting zoo is—let me guess." Zac tipped his head to one side as if he were listening to the faint whinny of nearby horses. "To the far left of the main house?"

"Actually, I think it's nearer the gate we arrived through, but you're not far off," Abby said, impressed with his ability to discern directions. "There's another kind of ring over there, though…"

"That's where Mandy teaches equestrian teams." Bonnie touched his arm. "You'll soon see it all for yourself, son. God will care for you and your eyes. Just be patient."

"Yeah." His mother's words seemed to douse whatever enthusiasm Zac had shown. He reached out with one hand. "Abby? Can we go inside?"

Though her heart ached for him and the uncertainty he faced, Abby said nothing as she slid her arm under his hand. She'd help him however she could. But she had to stop letting her emotions affect her. She was here to do a job for Zac. That was all. Then she'd leave.

"Three steps up to the veranda," she said softly. "Are you okay?"

"Yes." His voice dropped. "So not the triumphant homecoming I'd imagined having." Obviously hearing his mother's footsteps behind them, he muttered, "Better get used to it, huh?"

Abby didn't contradict him. She believed God had a plan, but nothing in her life had gone the way she thought it would and she guessed Zac was having the same experience. For once, she couldn't find words of reassurance. Because no one knew what his future held.

Nor hers.

Chapter Four

After three days of familiarizing himself with the inside of the log house, Zac's restlessness finally drove him out onto the deck, nearer the twins. He felt better when he was close to them. From the sound of their giggles they were below him, playing with their beloved dolls.

"Decided to join us?" Abby's cheerful voice chased away his gloomy thoughts.

"Maybe not exactly join." He grimaced, visualizing himself with a doll in each hand.

"You're here," Abby said brightly. "That's joining." The steps creaked. She must have moved onto the deck because her next words sounded much closer. "A lovely woman stopped by while you were snoozing. She'll be back after her riding lesson."

"Oh." Zac's stomach sank. "Did you catch a name?"

"Miss Partridge." Abby paused, then asked, "Isn't she the lady Drew mentioned? The former librarian?"

"Yes." *Oh, boy.* Zac swallowed hard.

"She seemed very nice, but perhaps a bit lonely," Abby mused. "Maybe she'll talk to you about it."

"Me?" he repeated, shocked by the thought.

"Yes, you. People talk to pastors or missionaries about lots of things, don't they? After all, your job in Africa was to offer people help in a confusing world, right? By talking to them?" She paused before adding, "Also, upstairs by my room there's a picture of you being awarded a counseling degree. Today Miss Partridge mentioned you used to counsel on some sort of help lines?"

"I did that as my practicum for my counseling degree. I got that degree as a way into medical school." Zac frowned, uneasy with the idea of Abby and Miss Partridge talking about him.

"I didn't chat with her long, but I found Miss Partridge very interesting. She's certainly knowledgeable about people around here." Her voice faded to a murmur. "It was like speaking to my own grandmother. If I had one."

"Did she mention why she wanted to see me?" he asked.

Abby chuckled. "You can ask her yourself because here she comes." She sounded pleased by the prospect.

Zac wasn't, but he forced his lips into a smile, anyway. Bonnie's lessons on hospitality had been drummed into his head years ago, and it wasn't easy to ignore them.

"Good morning, Zachary," the familiar voice from his youth rang out. "How are you? I do hope I'm not interrupting you, or Abigail or the children in some family moment?"

"No, we're just sitting here, having coffee. Please join us. Black, right?" *Good manners cost you nothing and are always in style*, Bonnie's voice reminded him. "How are you, Miss Partridge?"

"I'm fine as frog's hair, dear. And very happy you've come home. But no, I won't have coffee, thank you." Miss Partridge cleared her throat. "I have a matter to discuss with you, sir."

Uh-oh. Zac's shoulders tensed. What now?

"Girls, why don't we go get a drink?" Abby said. "You've been playing here for a while and you must be thirsty."

"I'm no—" Mia stopped in the middle of her protest.

Zac was pretty sure his daughter's sudden silence had something to do with Abby. He waited until the three had gone inside and silence reigned before he asked, "What can I do for you, ma'am?"

"Abby is a stunningly beautiful woman, young man. You're blessed to have her helping you."

"I agree." He waited, hoping she'd get to the point.

"I need a favor, Zac." He heard the creak of a chair and guessed the lady was getting more comfortable. "There's a man in our church," Miss Partridge began, then paused.

"Um, I'm not—"

"Please, hear me out." A sternness in the familiar voice made Zac stop protesting. There was no point, anyway, because they both knew he'd listen to whatever she had to say.

He swallowed his frustration, wishing he could see and thereby read expressions. He needed that advantage with Miss P., his private name for her.

"This man's name is Leo. He and his wife recently lost their unborn child." Miss P.'s voice grew soft, almost tender, something Zac hadn't heard before.

"Go on." He leaned forward, curious in spite of himself.

"Leo is now questioning everything. His grief is so deep he can't seem to find a way out. He's distanced himself from his wife, and of course she's grieving, too." Miss P.'s voice faltered. "You can imagine how he must feel, I'm sure, with two daughters of your own."

"You mean if Maria and I had lost either Mia

or Zoe." Zac shook his head. "Horrible, naturally. But grief is very deep and very personal. Usually you have to work your own way through it. Talking about it—well, it sometimes makes it feel worse."

"Nonsense," she proclaimed. "Talking about things with others helps us clarify, gain a new perspective from hearing someone else's point of view and hopefully learn how to channel our feelings and emotions into productive outlets."

The words were out before Zac could stop them. "Did you read that somewhere, Miss Partridge?"

"Why, yes. And it's also what you once told me," she shot back. "Isn't it true?"

"It can be," he agreed, choosing his words carefully. "But there's more to grief than that. It's not a matter of finding the right method to heal grief. There is no one way or one thing that can fix heartache. Grief is a process. You have to work through it."

"Talking to folks, helping them work through it, that is what you did." She sounded irritated.

"It is," he admitted. "But that was long ago, to complete a counseling degree as a prelude to med school. You already know all this," Zac reminded her. "Because you were the one who facilitated my studies."

"You had a bright mind and you needed stimulating," she said in flat, no-nonsense tone. "Psychology helped you think about others. You did good work when your father's friend mentored you in his psychological practice."

"Way back when," he agreed, determined to stick to his refusal. "Doesn't matter now."

The sound of a chair hitching forward on the wooden deck told Zac she'd moved closer. She'd always done that as a kind of pressure tactic, but before he could say a word, she resumed her argument.

"It does matter because you have both a counseling degree and a medical degree, Zachary." Starch laced her words. "Also, you're a missionary who has no doubt spoken to countless people about loss and death and other struggles."

Exactly what Abby had said.

"But I'm not a missionary anymore."

"I'm sure that losing your wife and then your mission is forcing you to deal with your own grief." Her words sounded softer now. "So surely you can empathize with Leo?"

"Miss Partridge." Zac thrust out his chin belligerently. He would not let her continue poking at his personal feelings.

"Please hear me out." Her voice dropped almost to a whisper. He had the strange thought that she had tears in her eyes. "You're a child of God. You know that He is with you, that He will lead you through the dark spots. That's what you told those you led to Him, isn't it?"

"Yes. But—"

"It must also be what you're telling yourself regarding your eyesight." Her warm hand slid atop his.

He sucked in his breath. Apparently there was no topic the lady wouldn't broach.

"And?" he demanded while his brain ordered, *Don't let her bully you!*

"I'm simply asking you to share a little bit of the light God's placed in your heart with this man who is in such deep pain."

"Why do you want so badly to help this Leo?" Her sensitivity confused Zac. He'd never thought of Miss P. as particularly compassionate.

"Because Leo's a fellow human being. Because he's hurting and because I think you have the words that could help him." She stopped, then spoke again more quickly. "Also because I said something to him that I shouldn't have and I'd like to make it up to him."

"I'm not sure you can do that." *Who among us hasn't spoken when we shouldn't have?* Zac felt his irritation melting. He was as guilty as anyone of misspeaking and then trying to fix the damage. But… "Leo needs to find his own way through."

"And if he can't?" Mis Partridge sighed. "I don't suppose you or I can fix things for him.

But at least we can be there if he needs us. Will you speak with him if he shows up here? Please?"

Zac didn't want to get involved in other people's problems. He was worn out with his own. He wanted peace and quiet to think about his world, the changes and what his future held. He wanted time to ask God why, to demand answers.

"Maybe if Leo can verbalize what he's feeling…" Miss P.'s heavy sigh told him she wouldn't give up easily.

"I'm not up to date in the field," Zac protested.

"Now that's not quite true," Miss Partridge challenged. "Your mother told me a year ago that you'd contacted your former mentor and asked him to forward some medical journals and texts regarding current counseling methods. She said you'd been doing a lot more of it as part of your outreach to needy souls who came to your mission seeking more than simply medical help."

"Yes, I was," he admitted. "But—"

"You are still qualified, aren't you?" she demanded.

"Yes, but—"

"Please think about it, Zac. And see what God has to say on the subject." Miss Partridge touched his shoulder. "I've been praying for years for your family and your work in Africa. I know it wasn't easy to serve there, and this most recent event has to be very hard. I can't fathom how difficult it must be to wait for God to heal your sight."

No more, his heart begged. *Please don't go there.*

And yet… Miss Partridge had been one of Zac's strongest supporters from the day he and Maria had left for Africa. She'd always sent a Christmas parcel with special items for each of them—the twins, Maria and him—carefully chosen to fit into the African culture, little things from home that he'd never mentioned missing but had. How thrilled they'd all been to receive her parcel that always arrived on time. She'd sent birthday cards and written newsy letters to inform about his parents and the ranch. Every year Miss Partridge had always spearheaded fundraising for the special projects he'd spoken about in his recorded presentations to his home church. Whether she knew it or not, Miss Partridge had been an integral part of the success of his and Maria's work.

Zac couldn't very well refuse this small request, no matter how little he wanted to do it.

"Our God is faithful, Zac. He knows your struggles and He is there for you," she was saying. What would she have to say if she knew how angry he was at God?

"Okay, I'll meet with Leo, but I can't promise anything."

"That will be wonderful, dear. I'll begin pray-

ing about it immediately." She sounded thrilled.
He wasn't.

"Shall I call Abby now?" he asked.

"Oh, no need to bother her, dear." He could tell
Miss Partridge rose by the way chair legs rasped
across the deck. "How did you, er, come to know
Abigail, Zac?"

And the lady was off again, prying into his
private business. Could a person inhale patience?

"I met Abby for the first time at the airport in
New York. She looked after the girls while I was
in the hospital. Since I wasn't allowed to travel to
get them, she brought them to meet me there," he
said, sounding chilly even to himself.

"But that's so romantic. Meeting a woman like
that in an airport? What a wonderful tale the two
of you will have in the years to come." It sounded
as if Miss P. wore boots as she thumped down the
stairs. "Isn't God simply incredible?" she called,
her voice growing fainter.

"Yeah." Zac would have glared at her retreat-
ing back, if he could have seen it. "Incredible."
A woman like that? What was that supposed to
mean? And *the years to come*? She made it sound
like they'd be together permanently.

"Are you okay?" Abby's tentative question
broke into his thoughts.

"I'm never sure after a talk with Miss P. She

leaves me…stunned," he concluded after searching for the right word.

"Daddy, we made cookies!" Mia sounded excited.

"Homemade cookies? Wow." He licked his lips in anticipation.

"Want one?" Zoe asked.

"Do crows fly?" He pushed his just-departed guest to the back of his mind. "I want more than one cookie."

"What kind of cookies are they, Abby?" Mia asked.

"They're a recipe my mom used to make. She called them *treathearts*. Here, try one." Her soft fingers pressed a still-warm, napkin-wrapped bundle into Zac's hand. "I brought fresh coffee to go with them."

"Thank you." He bit into the treat and let the flavors fill his mouth. "Chocolate, of course, sugar, coconut, oatmeal and…peanuts?" he guessed.

"Correct." As usual, Abby's voice sounded like she was smiling.

"They're delicious," he said. "Thank you, ladies."

"We're ladies," Mia squealed. "Hey. There's Ella. Let's go play fancy ladies with her."

Zac heard little feet thump down the stairs as the two jabbering voices grew fainter. His stomach tightened.

"Wait! Don't you two need to ask permission?" he called.

"But, Daddy, we're just going across the yard," Zoe protested.

"Yeah, Daddy, just the yard," Mia repeated.

"But I can't see that, girls, and I need to know when you leave and where you're going." He hated curtailing their freedom because fear dragged at him, but he was desperate to keep them safe. If he did, maybe this feeling of impending doom would lift.

"Abby can see us," Zoe argued.

Maybe that implied he didn't trust Abby? But that wasn't the case. Zac's frustration escalated, which must have been visible to his kids. Or maybe Abby gave them a warning look because the tone suddenly changed.

"Is it all right if we go play with Ella, Daddy?" Zoe now sounded uncertain and he hated that he'd caused it.

"Sure. But stay nearby," he muttered, disgusted with himself. "Don't wander away."

"Okay." With much clatter, the two girls dashed off, footsteps pounding on the hard ground.

"They're beginning to feel at home," Abby murmured. "It's a good idea to keep them busy. Drew's very careful with his daughter. Maybe your brother could teach the twins a little about riding the horses—"

"No!" Zac wouldn't let her go any further. "They're too young."

Abby didn't argue. She didn't repeat that Drew would never let the girls come to harm. Neither did she remind him that Ella, who was almost the same age as the twins, had learned how to ride a pony some time ago. She didn't mention that Ella was confident and self-assured on her horse or suggest that his daughters could be the same. Abby simply let it go.

And for that, Zac was extremely grateful.

Perhaps it was stupid that he couldn't explain why he was so determined to keep his daughters off the Double H horses. All he knew was that he lay awake at night beneath a dark oppressive cloud of fear that said God hadn't finished with him yet, that He had something else in store, something more difficult than anything Zac had yet gone through. Until that happened, he'd keep his daughters close. Zoe and Mia would just have to entertain themselves with something other than riding.

He heard the clink of Abby's coffee cup as she set it on the table.

"When you're finished here," he said, wondering whether she wished she hadn't come to the ranch, if she wanted to leave, "where will you go?"

"I haven't given it much thought. Why?" Her

calm, quiet tone never seemed to falter with uncertainty.

"Just wondered." The conversation threatened
to die there, and Zac didn't want that because he
didn't want to be alone right now. What he did
want was to know more about this inscrutable
woman. "You said you'll stay in the US for a
while?"

"Maybe. As a tourist," she said, a hint of a
smile in her voice. "I already miss Africa. It's
where my heart is."

"Because of Ken." He nodded. "I know. Maria's buried there, too. But I don't want to go back.
Not ever," he added fiercely.

"That's understandable," Abby murmured.
"Anyway, there's no point in going back for
Maria. She's in a better place."

He wondered why she hadn't said Ken was,
too.

"Actually, there's no point in me going back at
all." For once Zac didn't care that this was getting
too personal. Maybe talking to Abby would help.
"The mission was our dream, Maria's and mine.
We dreamed it together, built it together and
worked there together. We made tons of plans."

"I see," Abby murmured.

"But the worst part is…" Zac exhaled, the
weight of this admission like lead. "I was supposed to finish that dream, to make it come true. I

promised her I would. It will never happen now," he told her sorrowfully, mourning that loss anew.

"Which is not your fault, and which Maria would certainly understand," Abby insisted. "Will you tell me more about your work?" How did she manage to sound so interested?

"I don't want to dwell on it now," Zac mumbled. "Let's talk about something else."

"Sure." Abby's silence lasted barely a second. "Miss Partridge?"

"Not my favorite subject, either." He grimaced. "She wants me to talk to some fellow named Leo who just lost an unborn child."

Abby gasped. "Oh, how sad." Then in the next breath she asked, "Why you?"

"It's a long story."

"I have time." Abby said no more. He had the sense that she leaned back, waiting.

"I finished high school before my sixteenth birthday." Zac could hear her huff of surprise. "I told you Drew and I were nerds. Anyway, I was bored and I had a lot of spare time. I spent some of it at the library, helping a buddy of mine finish his studies so he could graduate. I didn't realize Miss P. was listening to us."

"Sounds interesting." Abby's unspoken curiosity made him chuckle.

"That's a nice word for eavesdropping. Anyway, later Miss P. invited me to hear a speaker at the library. Turned out he was Ben's client, a psychologist who'd come to the ranch many times to hike." Zac could still visualize that round face with its wise eyes peering at him.

"Go on," Abby encouraged.

"Dr. Dave could get anyone to talk, including me. He got my dad to agree to an overnight campout where he coaxed me into pouring out my dream of medicine. It was Dr. Dave who suggested I begin studying for a counseling degree through distance education with him as my mentor, while I waited to get into college. He said it would show serious intent and, because of the science requirements, might even be allowed as a premed degree." He shrugged. "Miss Partridge used her library connections and helped me figure out how to do it."

"Wasn't that kind of her?"

Looking back, Zac had to agree.

"Very kind," he said with a chuckle. "Even if she did set herself up as my taskmaster. Thanks to her grilling, I absorbed a lot of stuff I might never have learned till med school. Also thanks to her, I never turned in a late assignment."

"How does this relate to Leo?" she wondered.

"I needed to do a practicum to get my master's in counseling. Dr. Dave invited me to live with him and work under him for a year. I got hooked on talking to people and racked up more hours counseling than any other master's student. Turns out, that's what fast-tracked me into medical school at nineteen."

"So counseling comes naturally to you." Abby sounded impressed, but he didn't want her to get the wrong idea.

"I didn't do much after that, just the stuff we were required to do during training and residency. But in Africa, at our mission in the boonies, we didn't have psychiatrists or psychologists so I either had to manage the best I could or send folks to the city. Most couldn't afford to go or wouldn't leave because of family commitments, so last year I got back into counseling. I asked Dr. Dave to send me as much material as he could so I could catch up with current views and methods. We'd begun to get a lot of people coming to the mission who had lost family in traumatic circumstances and wanted to talk about it. So…" His voice trailed away.

"So you helped them," Abby finished. "Amazing."

"It's a much different experience than medicine. More intuitive, I guess. What goes on inside human heads is fascinating. Talking with folks gave me a welcome break from the medical stuff I'd been doing." He shrugged. "Turns out my mom blabbed about my brushing up on counseling to Miss P. and now she thinks I'm the perfect person to talk Leo through his grief."

"Is that what she said?" Abby asked.

Zac mentally replayed the conversation.

"No," he finally admitted. "She just asked me to talk to him. But I doubt counseling him would be anything like what I did in Africa."

"Isn't the basis of counseling listening? Maybe Miss Partridge realizes that what Leo really needs is someone to listen to him," Abby said thoughtfully. "Sometimes the kids that came to me— never mind."

"No, please continue." Surprised by how much he wanted to hear her thoughts, Zac inclined his head and waited for her to explain.

"Of course it's not the same as what you did or Leo's issues. Many of the children who came to me were running from danger and were so terrified about what had happened that they kept themselves locked up tight." It was obvious Abby was remembering specific cases.

"Understandable reactions for anyone who's gone through horrible situations." He nodded, thinking about his own reactions.

"I never pressed them because I didn't want to make them sad or force them to relive their pain. But it would always come out, sometimes bit by bit, sometimes in a rush of weeping and sometimes in a whisper, as if they were afraid to say the actual words but desperately needed the release." Her voice lightened. "I guess we all need someone to confide in once in a while."

Inherent in her comment was, *Even you, Zac.*

He pushed it away. He did not want to talk about his memories of that black day when he'd lost his sight. Not with Abby, not with anyone.

Except perhaps with God, to ask why He'd allowed it.

A week later Abby sat on the lawn in front of the log house, enjoying the afternoon sun on her skin as she demonstrated how to make dandelion necklaces to Mia and Zoe. She hoped to keep them interested in something for perhaps an hour or so. But it was getting difficult to keep them entertained and busy enough so that Zac could hear them without being bothered by their noise.

The three of them all looked up when a half-ton truck pulled into the driveway. A man in his early thirties climbed out, a desperate weariness reflected in the slump of his shoulders and his preoccupied gaze around the yard.

"Hello," she called when it looked as if he was searching for something. "Can I help you?"

"Miss Partridge said—that is, uh…" His face reddened.

"Are you Leo?" Abby's heart welled with sadness when he nodded. "You'll want Zac. He's inside. Come, I'll introduce you. I'm Abby, by the way. Zac's nurse." She rose and introduced the twins, then told them to remain where they were until she returned. As she walked with Leo toward the house, she tried to prepare him. "Zac is recovering from some eye injuries so he won't be able to actually see you," she warned.

"Miss Partridge told me." He stopped, hesitated. "Maybe I shouldn't bother him—"

"Oh, please stay. I think his injuries make him a bit lonely," she said, lowering her voice as she led the way up the stairs. She tapped on the door once, then peeked inside. "Zac? Leo is here wondering if you have a moment to speak with him."

Zac had been sprawled on the sofa, hands behind his head. But at her words he sat up, swung his legs around and planted his feet on the floor.

"Come on in, Leo," he called. "Have a seat. Want a cup of coffee?"

"Sure. Thanks." Leo studied Zac for a few seconds before choosing a seat across from him. "Thank you," he said when Abby handed him a steaming mug. "Black is perfect."

"Anything else I can get?" She glanced from one man to the other. "Coffee for you, Zac?"

"Just a glass of water, please," he said quietly. The fast swallow and his hand feeling for the cushion beside him told her he was nervous.

"Here you are." She placed the glass in his

hand and smiled at Leo. "If you're good to go, the girls and I will be outside. It's so lovely I think we'll go on a treasure hunt." She'd only just made up the idea, but Zac didn't need to know that. Something told her he needed time and privacy to concentrate on the other man. "See you, Leo."

"Nice to meet you, Abby. Thanks."

"No problem." When she stepped outside, the twins were nowhere to be seen. Abby's heart stopped for a minute until she spied them talking to their grandmother on the deck of the main house. She walked over, trying to decide the best way to reprimand the two spirited girls for disobeying. In the end she didn't have to.

"We came over here without asking." Mia hung her head. "I'm sorry, Abby."

"Me, too." Zoe's chin thrust up defiantly. "But we wanted to talk to our grandma."

"Oh, Abby, I'm so sorry. I didn't realize you'd told them to stay where they were." Bonnie surveyed the twins with a serious expression. "Obeying the rules is very important on a ranch, girls. We need to know you're exactly where you're supposed to be."

"Why?" That was Zoe, always the bold one.

"So that you won't get hurt." Abby stepped in. "We can't always explain why to you, Zoe. But you must obey. Otherwise I am going to have to restrict you."

"We'll obey," the twins said in unison. "We promise."

"I'm sorry, Abby." Zoe did indeed look repentant.

"I forgive you, sweetheart." She kept her voice firm even though her heart weakened at their sweet smiles. "Sorry means you won't do it again, right?"

"Right," they chirped.

"I'm glad you understand that obedience is important." Bonnie smiled at both before glancing at Abby. "Now, would it be okay for you all to visit my petting zoo?"

"I'd love it." Abby tucked away her treasure hunt plans for another day. "Girls?"

"Yes, please," they responded, again in unison, eager smiles wreathing their faces.

Ten minutes later Abby leaned against a fence rail beside Bonnie, chuckling as the excited sisters scurried around, scattering seed for the chickens to eat.

"Tell me about yourself, Abby. I'm sorry we haven't had more time to chat since you arrived." Bonnie laughed when the girls shrieked as an old rooster raced toward them. "Zac said you're a widow?"

"Yes." Abby gave the barest bones explanation about the deaths of her husband and son and her life following.

"How awful! I'm so sorry, dear." Bonnie, eyes

teary, embraced her. "And then out of your grief came your children's ministry. How amazing."

Encouraged, Abby told her about the kids she'd hosted. When she realized she was talking too much, she quickly turned the conversation back to Bonnie and her adopted sons.

"Taking on three young boys must have been challenging."

"But such a blessing. Ben and I adored every moment. Having the boys return home again is even better." Again Bonnie's eyes welled with tears.

"I'm sure you missed Zac, Maria and the twins," Abby said consolingly.

"Oh, we did! So much. But we sacrificed willingly, knowing how important their ministry was both to them and to Africa. We are so proud of our son." Her eyes grew sad and her voice snagged in her throat as she whispered, "I suppose that's why it's so difficult to see Zac the way he is now, aimless, his mission gone, frightened about his eyesight. He doesn't seem interested in his future at all." Bonnie sighed. "It's hard to understand God's ways sometimes."

"Yes, it is," Abby agreed fervently.

"And yet we must trust that our Father knows best." Bonnie regained her composure and smiled. "What about your future, Abby? You're very beautiful. Don't you want to marry again?" Bonnie asked.

"No." Abby shook her head firmly.

"I understand. But in time your grief will pass." Bonnie touched her shoulder. "The pain does lessen with time."

"I don't want it to. I don't want to ever forget my marriage." Abby knew she sounded strange, but she didn't care. She needed to say it out loud, to remind herself that she had to quash any and all soft thoughts about Zac. "Girls," she called, hoping to forestall the questions she saw building on Bonnie's face. "Remember to ask permission before opening a gate."

Bonnie agreed Mia and Zoe could enter the pen that held six chocolate lab puppies. The twins oohed and ahhed over the animals as they flopped down on the grass. They burst into giggles as pink tongues licked their faces.

"I'm like the local pet shelter," Bonnie explained. "I try to ensure that unwanted, found, injured or otherwise displaced animals are given good homes where they will be cared for. I can't turn any needy animal away."

"It's wonderful." Abby couldn't believe the number and variety of animals around them and was about to ask a question about them when Bonnie changed the subject.

"I'm so glad you agreed to stay awhile to help Zac. I'm praying your sunny spirit and cheery ways will help him overcome the negativity that has him in its grip."

"I'm sure the uncertainty of not knowing what will happen with his sight must be daunting," Abby murmured.

"Yes, but I've never seen him so negative about God. It worries me," Bonnie admitted. "I'll keep praying God will send him a new task to help get his mind off his own situation."

Abby didn't tell her that it might already be happening with Leo.

"I'd better find Ben," Bonnie said after a glance at her watch. "Miss Partridge is taking us to get our dressings changed. It's a long drive."

"I could change them for you, if you like," Abby volunteered, thinking that here at last was something she could do to repay these wonderful people. "That's if your doctor agrees, and if you want me to."

"How very generous of you, my dear. It would be a great relief not to have to trouble Miss Partridge to make these trips so often." Bonnie smiled. "I'll speak to Dr. Metcalfe about it today. Do you mind if he calls you at our place?"

"Not at all. I'd be glad to speak to him, and to help you and Ben however I can," Abby assured her. "You only have to ask. It's the least I can do. You've both been so generous to me."

"It's our pleasure. Well, time to go." Bonnie's

smile widened as the twins regretfully released the puppies and exited the petting zoo. "You can always come back," she promised them.

They all waved goodbye as Miss Partridge drove the couple away a few moments later, then reluctantly returned to their dandelion necklaces. Abby couldn't help wondering how Zac's conversation was going. Her concerns ballooned when Leo emerged from the house a short time later with his head tucked into his shoulders. Hadn't Zac been able to help him?

"Abby?"

"Yes, Zoe?" She smiled at the two sweet children who'd captured her heart the first day they'd arrived in her home.

Normally Abby refused to allow herself to bond so closely with children, certainly not immediately. Losing Levi had made her protect her emotions. Oddly, she'd felt an immediate and very strong connection with the Calhoun girls.

"Why won't Daddy let me and Mia ride the horses?" Zoe demanded with a frown. "Ella rides."

"You'd have to ask him." Abby wasn't going to criticize Zac, and yet she didn't want the twins pressing him when he still wasn't comfortable with letting them go far from him. "Sometimes parents make rules for your good that they can't explain to you."

"Like when God says in the Bible that we're

not supposed to lie and doesn't say why not?" Zoe wondered.

"Sort of like that." Abby found all kids' simplicity irresistible, but especially these two. "I'm sure that eventually your father will teach you to ride the horses, but right now, with his eye problems, he can't see if you get in trouble and he can't see to help you. Your daddy doesn't want you to get hurt, girls. He loves you too much."

"But Uncle Drew could—"

"Honey, I think your daddy wants to be the one to teach you how to ride horses." Abby brushed their dark heads consolingly. "Perhaps he wants to make it a very special time when you'll do it as a family. Together. Does that make sense?"

"I guess." Mia and Zoe looked at each other and shrugged, accepting her explanation. For now. "I'm hungry. Can we go make cookies again? All the other ones got eaten up."

"Maybe we'll chop some fresh vegetables to make soup for supper," Abby suggested. "If you're hungry, you can each have a glass of milk and then you won't be too full to eat a good meal."

"I like soup." Mia grinned.

"I like cookies better," Zoe chimed in with a grin. "But maybe not for supper."

Abby helped them clean up their mess, then watched as the twins raced up the stairs and into their new home, calling out excitedly to their father. They were so full of life and boundless energy. But they needed more to do. She allowed them some time to tell Zac about the petting zoo before following.

How could she phrase her questions about Zac's discussion with Leo?

I'm here, Lord, she prayed silently. *Show me what to do to help this family. And Zac.*

Once the vegetables were chopped and simmering on the stove, the twins had gone to their room to play with their dolls until supper, and Abby had tidied the kitchen and prepared biscuits to go with the soup, she finally sat down across from Zac.

"So? How did it go with Leo?" she asked.

"I'm not sure I was much help," Zac said, defeat echoing through his words. "There are said to be five stages of grief. In my opinion Leo is through the first two."

"Denial and anger, if I remember correctly," Abby murmured.

"Yes." Zac looked carelessly handsome as he lounged on the tan leather sofa, his head tilted upward, one hank of hair flopping over his covered left eye. "He's heavy into bargaining now. 'If I did this or made amends for that, maybe God would undo what He's done.' Leo knows it isn't true, but he's struggling to find a way out. I wish

I had some of my old college texts. And I wish I could see to read them," he added with a grimace.

"You want to keep refreshing your knowledge?" she guessed.

"Because I'm out of step. Counseling methods have changed." His chiseled face tightened. "I'd like to help the guy if I could. But how? I don't really know what to tell him."

"People are people all over the world, Zac. You're a doctor and a missionary." Abby kept her voice light. "Your work encompasses body, mind and spirit. Doesn't it?"

"Yes, but—"

"I have an idea." Abby had been longing for someone to give her a specific list of tasks to complete, a goal to strive for so that her thoughts wouldn't keep returning to the past, reviving the same old questions about how she'd failed at marriage. Maybe Zac's issues could offer the diversion she craved. "What if we contacted your Dr. Dave and got some more information from him, like studies or papers that deal with grief?"

"Good idea," Zac agreed, then added in a droll tone, "Only I can't see to read them."

"I can," she said, excited by the prospect. "I could read them aloud to you after the girls are tucked in for the night. Would that help?"

"It's a very generous offer," he said immediately. "But—"

"Please, Zac. Just accept," she begged. "Otherwise I am going to be bored to tears with nothing much to do."

"But it's not part of your job," he protested.

"My job is to help however I can," she insisted. "I do as much as I can for your parents, but I don't think your mother wants me hovering over her too much. She's finding satisfaction in accomplishing things for herself as she heals, which is perfectly normal. Anyway, I really want to do this."

It didn't matter how much Zac tried to dissuade her. Abby had caught just the barest tinge of hope in his voice and she intended to build on that.

"When we were first married, Ken didn't like my nursing hours so I cut back, but I kept active with volunteer work." Abby chose her words carefully. "I hate sitting around. I need to feel useful."

"It's kind of you, but you're already watching the twins," Zac argued.

"They don't require much watching, though I think we'll have to make a trip to the town library." She exhaled. "I'm happy to do whatever needs to be done around here, including read to you, if it's helpful. But if all you need is someone to watch the girls, apply your drops and change the dressings, a nanny and a community nurse are your answer. I *need* to do more, Zac. Otherwise I'm afraid I'll start feeling homesick."

"I didn't realize…" It took Zac less than ten seconds to decide. "If you're sure you want to do it, and you promise to let me know if it becomes too onerous, I'll gladly accept your help, Abby." He thrust out his hand. "Thank you."

"You're very welcome."

As Zac's strong fingers gripped hers, Abby felt a zap of connection shiver up her arm. At the same time a warning whispered inside her head.

Careful.

Chapter Five

Two days later, from his chair on the deck of his home, Zac unabashedly eavesdropped on Miss Partridge and Abby, who were chatting around the corner of the house. The former had apparently just finished her riding lesson with Mandy.

"It's such fun on that horse, Abby, I don't know why I waited so long to do it," Miss Partridge said. "You should get those two young girls up on horseback, too."

"I'm sure Zac will see to that at the right time," came Abby's quiet response.

"It's always easiest to start young," the lady pronounced. "Anyway, I hope these are the books Dr. Dave requested."

"You've made a good start." It seemed to Zac that a smile always wove through Abby's words. "Thank you so much for getting these so quickly."

"My pleasure. Reminds me of the old days

when I used to get him books for his schooling. How's Leo doing?" Miss Partridge asked in a quick subject change.

"I don't know. The discussions between him and Zac are private."

"And I shouldn't ask." Miss P. chuckled. "I won't, though I will say Leo looks worse than before. I was hoping Zac could help him but…"

"These things take time. Losing a child is very difficult." Abby stopped suddenly.

Zac heard the not-quite-hidden pain underlying her words and realized she was remembering her own lost boy. Compassion for this hurting mother mushroomed inside him. Somehow he never thought of Abby as mourning, and yet she must be.

"The death of a child would challenge one's faith in a good God," Miss Partridge agreed. "I do hope Leo is healing."

"I know Zac will do what he can." Abby's confidence sent a frisson of pleasure through Zac.

"Now about the community family night this evening. You are coming, aren't you, Abby?"

Zac recalled that Miss Partridge had been in charge of family nights even when he was a teen, though he'd never understood why a single woman without children would have that task. Still, he had to admit she had a gift for making those get-togethers memorable. Also, Miss

P. used the event as an excuse to visit older folks around the community, encouraging them to attend while learning if they needed anything.

"I think the family should go without me," Abby demurred. "I have some thank-you notes I should write to folks back home."

"Write them tomorrow," the former librarian ordered. He could almost visualize Miss P.'s fingers fluttering through the air in a motion that said Abby's letters weren't as urgent as family night. "You mustn't miss this opportunity to familiarize yourself with folks in Sunshine. It's a fantastic community."

"I'm sure it is, but—oh, hello, Zac." Abby seemed surprised that he'd managed to find his way to the edge of the deck, just above where they were standing. "Did our gabbing wake you?"

"I wasn't sleeping." He was disgusted. Did he look like he needed a morning nap? "Hello, Miss P. Yes, we'll be there tonight, I'm sure. Though we might have to find a driver."

"Well, you let me know if you do. I have a list of drivers. It's going to be so fun." The woman laughed gaily. "I must get going. Things to do, people to see and all that jazz. Ta ta, dears."

"You don't have to find a driver. I have an international driving license." Abby's footsteps on wood alerted him that she was joining him on the deck. "I just love that woman."

"Love? Miss P.?" Zac startled. "Why?"

"She has such a zest for life. Projects and plans galore. She bounces from one to the next." Something thudded, probably the books Abby had received from Miss Partridge. "She gives new meaning to aging gracefully."

"Huh. Never thought of her that way." He accepted Abby's offer of iced tea and when she returned with it asked, "Where are the twins?"

"Guess." Abby's lilting voice made Zac think she'd be as lively as Miss P. when she aged.

"I don't really like guessing. I like *knowing* things," he said with a frown.

"Ain't that the truth?" There was a tinkle as Abby set down her glass. She sighed. "The girls are helping your mom in her flower garden, Zac, but you must pretend you don't know anything about it."

"Why?" Zac wondered.

"Because they want to surprise you." He knew she'd moved to the porch swing because of the rhythmic creak. "It's so beautiful here."

"You're not homesick for Africa?" He was reminded of what she'd said before about needing to keep busy.

"Sometimes. Mostly for the heat when those mountains send a chill down after midnight," she teased. "But honestly, it's hard to stay homesick in a gorgeous place like this. The sky is such a rich clear blue. The mountains' pretty top hats of snow and the sparkling waterfalls that tumble down their ragged sides take my breath away. The lushness of Peace Meadow just invites you to relax in it. There are such pretty wildflowers strewn across hill and dale. If I were a painter, I'd commit this view to canvas for all the world to appreciate."

"You have quite a way with words." He could tell Abby was embarrassed by her loquaciousness.

"Being here makes you appreciate God's magnificent creation. Seeing the horses and cattle roam those luxurious green fields and smelling that freshly mown grass Drew cut this morning—it's the light and the warmth and the people. It's…everything, I guess," she finished, sounding sheepish.

"I'm glad you're enjoying yourself. I was hoping you wouldn't become bored too quickly." Saying that made Zac sound unappreciative for the ranch, and he wasn't. He simply couldn't get past his frustration at what he'd lost. "What books did Miss P. bring?" He nodded as she read the titles. "That's a good start. But I hate that reading them to me will take away from your free time." He'd tried and failed to figure out another alternative on his own.

"I wouldn't have said I wanted to do it if I

didn't," Abby chided. "Let's not second-guess that decision. Now, you should know that I intend to go to town with Mandy this afternoon to get some groceries. Anything you need? I'll take the twins along. Leo's coming again, isn't he?"

"So he said." Zac sighed. "You know, I'm not sure this whole counseling thing is a good idea. What if I can't help him?"

"Maybe you can't. Maybe you're not supposed to," came Abby's calm response.

"Then why...?" He blinked in confusion, wishing for the hundredth time that he could see her expression.

"Maybe what Leo needs most isn't someone who thinks they have to have all the answers. Maybe he really needs someone to just listen to him. You *can* do that, Zac."

"Yes, but I don't want to say the wrong thing or cause him more pain than he's in," he shot back in irritation. "I feel like I'm walking a tightrope around him."

"You're thinking about yourself too much. It's not about you, Zac. It's about Leo and *his* pain." Abby's quiet chiding held his attention. "Try to forget yourself and focus on him and his needs. Anyway, you know all that," she said. "Counseling isn't new to you."

"No, you're right," he said, considering her words. "It isn't about me."

"I think we as Christians often do that," she said, sounding as if her thoughts were on something far away. "We get focused on our own problems in our own little world and we don't see that God put us where we are because there are hurting people all around us who need us to care about them." Her words echoed around the covered deck. "At least, that's what I've found. My issues dissolve when I think about the other person and what they need."

"Which is how you were able to minister to such needy kids." Zac knew it was true. "You put your mind to making their world better."

"And, in the process, improved my own," she added cheerfully. "Until—" It went suddenly silent on the deck. Abby must have risen because he heard the screen door creak open. "I'd better get lunch started," she said hurriedly just before the door slammed.

Stupid. Zac reamed himself out for not tiptoeing around the memory of her husband and son. Of course Abby couldn't forget about their deaths any more than he could forget about Maria's.

He lifted his foot to rest it on the coffee table. As he did so, his shoe bumped a book. He reached out, let his fingertips outline the hard binding and thin pages.

For a moment he considered moving the coverings over his eyes just enough to test whether or not he could see the words on the page. But the sounds of the twins returning nixed that thought. Maybe he'd try to see something, like her face, next time Abby changed his dressings. He desperately wanted to know if he'd ever be able to see again.

And if I can't? What then?

Uncomfortable with that question, Zac sat up straight.

"Zoe. Mia. Come and tell me what you've been doing."

The girls tried to keep their secret of planting seeds with Bonnie, but in their excited chatter they quickly gave away their surprise. Listening to them helped dim his dark thoughts for a while. But when Abby called them in for lunch, Zac knew there would be no permanent escape. Eventually he'd have to face his worst fear.

What are You doing, God? he demanded silently as he negotiated his way to the table. *Why is this happening to me?*

God, it seemed, was not ready to explain.

"I'm sorry I've been neglecting you," Mandy apologized as she drove Abby and the twins into town two hours later. "I just get so bogged down sometimes."

"Don't apologize." Abby shook her head. "You have a life to get on with and we can't upset that.

If you'd give me something to do, I'd gladly do it. I'd love to help out in any way you need." She shrugged. "But don't worry about us. We've been familiarizing ourselves with the ranch. The girls are loving it."

"Hanging Hearts Ranch is so fun, Auntie Mandy." Zoe giggled when Ella tickled her.

"Yeah, fun," her sister repeated.

"So you're not bored?" Mandy said with a wink at Abby.

"What's bored, Mama?" Ella spared her mother a scant second for the reply before turning her focus back on her doll. "Never mind."

Abby and Mandy shared a grin.

"I certainly am not bored," Abby assured her. "The ranch is gorgeous and there's so much to see. Yesterday I went for a walk behind Zac's place and found this wonderful little meadow full of wildflowers. Peace Meadow, Bonnie called it. What an unusual name."

"That's what we've called it since we were kids. Bonnie and Ben used to hold huge picnics there. Everyone brought food and chairs and we'd have a campfire. My friends and I used to sun-bathe there and pick the wildflowers. Drew, Zac and Ben often tossed a football there, too. It's a great spot."

"Hmm, maybe my idea won't work, then." Abby chewed her bottom lip.

"What idea?" Mandy parked in front of the general store.

"Well, you know that Zac is spending time with a man named Leo who recently lost a child?" She waited for Mandy's nod. "It's not the easiest thing to get some private time and space inside the cabin. I try to keep the girls busy outdoors so the men can talk freely, but you know how kids are."

"Yes, I do. And the last couple of rainy days must have made it even more difficult. So you believe Peace Meadow would be a good place for Zac and his guest to talk without interruption?" Mandy's smile filled her face. "It's a great idea, though I'm pretty sure they'd prefer some chairs to sit on rather than the old stumps we used as kids. I wonder what ever happened to the two Adirondack chairs that Ben made long ago?"

"I didn't see any chairs yesterday," Abby murmured as she mentally scanned the meadow.

"They've probably disintegrated after all these years. But maybe we can find some here that would work." Mandy waved a hand toward the general store. "This place offers a wide variety of stuff."

"We can look." Abby exited the car slowly, worried about taking the excited twins into a store with a huge display of glass ornaments right at the entrance.

"Come on. They have a place for kids to play," Ella urged Mia and Zoe. "It's cool."

"You look nervous." Mandy held the door open for the girls to enter, then smiled at Abby. "Don't be. They'll be fine in the kids' area, and that means we can look as long as we want."

Abby wasn't exactly sure she wanted to spend much time in a hardware store, until she saw the extensive stock it carried and realized there were a number of things she needed—some jeans and a couple of Western shirts, new sunhats for the twins, as well as some kitchen utensils and a couple of insulated mugs Zac could use if he went to the meadow. Her cart filled rapidly, but when she was about to pick up a big ball of white rope, Mandy stopped her.

"We have plenty of that on the ranch, Abby," she said. "For whatever you need."

"Okay." She blinked. Mandy's basket was heaped with sewing supplies. "Do you make clothes for Ella?"

"No. Quilts. Bonnie and I usually have a project going so if it gets really hot—or really cold in the winter—and we need some chat time, we can sit down and stitch together." Mandy shrugged. "Then we give them away to our church's graduating students or families in need or new babies or—the list is endless."

"Do you make a lot of quilts?" Abby was intrigued.

"Quite a few." Mandy laughed. "You might say we're addicted to quilting. You're welcome to join us if you want. It's not hard to learn."

"I'd like to, if you think I can do it." She smiled at Mandy's enthusiastic nod but something puzzled her. "How does Bonnie manage now with her burned hands?"

"She struggles." Mandy's expression grew serious. "But it's something she loves and she refuses to give it up. She cuts everything and does most of the machine stitching because it's easier for her. The hand stitching isn't, but I actually think it's helping her dexterity."

"How wonderful. I've never done anything like quilting, though in Botswana the ladies did some incredible stitchwork. I bought a huge wall hanging a few years ago from a woman who created the entire picture from an idea in her head. All handmade."

"I'd love to see it." Mandy pushed her cart behind Abby into the checkout line.

"It should be coming with my trunk, soon, I hope." As Abby loaded her items on the counter for the clerk to ring up, she felt a pang of loneliness for the land she loved. She pulled out her credit card as a voice from the past chided, *You waste so much money on silly things, Abigail.*

*Things you don't need, like toys for children who
aren't even yours. Don't they have enough toys?*

This from a man who wanted money to buy
a newer, fancier airplane. No, she would not go
back to the tension and fear, to denying herself
something she loved simply to appease Ken. She
was free now. Free to live her life the way she
wanted, to savor precious intangibles as well as
things that brought her joy. As if to reinforce that,
she added two small bags of peppermints to her
stash.

While Mandy paid for her things, Abby followed the sound of giggles to a fenced-off corner
at the back of the store where the three girls were
deeply engaged in a board game with purple hip-
popotamuses. She watched for several minutes
before they noticed her.

"I'm winning, Abby," Zoe proclaimed, sacri-
ficing a move in order for Mia's hippo to escape
the swamp.

Then Ella rolled a six which catapulted her
over the finish line. "Good game," she cheered
as she high-fived the other two.

"Mandy's almost ready to leave so I think
you'd better put away the game," Abby said. She
needn't have bothered because the girls were already restoring order to the small space under
Ella's direction.

"We hafta make it right," she told them.

"Why?" Mia wondered.

"So it's ready for the next kid to play. Then they clean up and when we come next time it's ready for us. It's called—" She stopped short, thought a moment then said triumphantly, "Co-operation."

"Very good, Ella. I'm proud of you girls." And Abby was. As proud as any mother would be. If only...

"Are we ready to hit the library now?" Mandy asked from behind Abby.

"Yes!" Ella squealed. Mia and Zoe frowned at her in confusion. "We go there to get storybooks that we c'n read at home. Don't 'cha know what a library is?"

The twins shook their heads slowly.

"We didn't have that in our village," Mia explained.

"But we like books," Zoe said.

"The library's got lots of 'em," Ella told her.

"We'll head over there right away," Mandy promised. "But first I saw something I need to show you, Abby. I'd like your opinion. Come along, girls, and don't touch." She led the way around the kids' area and through a side door into a covered annex filled with half-unpacked lawn and patio furniture. "Voilà!" she pronounced, pointing.

Abby blinked in surprise at the brightly colored Adirondack chairs stacked nearby.

"They're made of some composite material so they won't need painting, won't fade from the sun and don't need cushions," Mandy explained. "There are also side tables."

"An' chairs for us." Zoe immediately plopped down into a brilliant pink pint-sized chair. The other girls followed, Mia in a baby-blue chair and Ella in a yellow one.

"What do you think, Abby?" Mandy studied her, a huge grin on her face.

"I think they're perfect." Abby made the decision in an instant. "Can I buy six of them?"

"Why six?" Mandy wondered.

"Make that eight. Three Calhouns and any women they bring along makes six." She winked at Mandy. "Add two for Ben and Bonnie."

"What about kids?" Ella demanded.

"Okay, four kids' chairs, too, in case someone adds to the family," Abby said with a wink at her new friend. "I also think we need a picnic table because Peace Meadow is perfect for picnics." She stopped, suddenly aware of Mandy's surprise. Doubt immediately took over. "Is it too much? Is it presumptuous of me to buy them? I mean, I know it's not my place, but I thought if Zac and his guests felt comfortable it would make it easier—"

"Abby, stop." Mandy laid a hand on her shoulder. "It's a wonderful idea. I can just picture everything. We'll all use that space so much more. I don't know why I never thought of it. But you're our guest. You can't pay."

"I want to." Abby decided it was time to confide in Mandy. "Zac is so sure he will be useless at listening to and helping Leo. I'm sure he can do it, but he needs to relax. Me bursting in to wash grubby children's hands or get a snack must make it difficult for Leo to really open up." She paused, then lowered her voice. "Zac needs to find a different way to minister to people. I have a hunch that sitting in that gorgeous meadow, where it's so peaceful and where he can be alone with his thoughts sometimes, would help both him and whomever comes to see him. Is that silly?"

Mandy smiled and shook her head. "Not silly at all. Just very thoughtful and kind and caring. You choose whatever you think is appropriate. As the ranch manager, I'll authorize payment for whatever items you decide on."

"But I don't want to cause Hanging Hearts any expense," Abby protested. "I just want to help, to be part of something."

"You have helped, Abby. You are part of us. It's a wonderful idea. But I insist the ranch pays for the furniture." Mandy's voice dropped. "We'll go to the library while you choose whatever's appropriate. I'd help you but my world is ranching, not decorating. I know you'll choose exactly what the meadow needs. And let's keep the makeover a secret until you decide to unveil it." She summoned the girls. "See you in a bit," she said, and winked before shepherding them out of the building.

Abby stood there, shocked, surprised and a little uncertain about carrying through her idea. But then a mental image floated through her head of Zac's face this morning when he'd been doubting himself. That decided it for her and she went to find the store manager.

There was so little she could do for this family. Creating a special space seemed like a small thing, but she'd pray it rendered big dividends for the widower and his future.

"I think I'd prefer to stay here and attend to some chores," Abby argued when they'd finished supper later that night. But Zac wasn't taking no for an answer.

"Family nights are a big deal in this community," he said, wiping dry each dish she put into his hands. "You have to go. Besides, I'll need help to get around."

That was doubtful. The community center hadn't changed one iota in past years and he'd known the place like the back of his hand. But if guilt worked, he'd use it.

"Well." Great! Abby was actually thinking about it.

"Come on, Abby. Pull on a pair of jeans and a T-shirt and join in the fun. You read those dry old texts to me for two hours last night. You deserve a break."

"All right. I'll go, but only because I bought some jeans today. Otherwise I'd have nothing to wear." She rolled her eyes when he complained he'd heard that before. "I hope they don't look stupid on me. I've never worn jeans and Mandy wasn't much help in telling me if they are in style."

"Mandy doesn't do style. She does comfort. And she always looks great," Zac stated. Then he frowned. "You've never worn jeans? Really?"

"My boarding school didn't allow them, and anyway, it was usually too warm for jeans," she said. "Also, Ken—he didn't like me wearing jeans. He said they weren't feminine." The smile had leeched from her voice. Now she sounded sad. Zac needed to change that.

"I wish I could have a chat with Ken," he muttered, then lightened up. "Thing is, you're in Montana now. Everybody wears jeans. I'll finish drying these dishes. You go get ready." As an afterthought he asked, "What are the twins wearing?"

"T-shirts and chinos. Their hoodies are hanging by the door." She paused. He could sense her hesitation. "Are you positive I should go?"

"Positively positive." He grinned. "Also, Miss P. would have my head if you didn't."

Drew picked them up ten minutes later with Ella in tow.

"Mandy's driving Ma and Dad in," he said as he waited for Zac to get his light jacket.

"Where's Abby?" Surely she hadn't backed out?

"Belting the twins into the car." Drew straightened his brother's collar.

"Can I ask you something?" Zac wondered if this was a mistake. He didn't want to give the wrong impression but he needed to know.

"Don't like the sound of that," his brother mumbled. "But go ahead."

"When you picked us up at the airport, it seemed to me like you had a weird reaction to Abby. Why?"

For a few minutes Drew said nothing, and Zac wondered what was wrong. Then, after exhaling heavily, the response came.

"I keep forgetting you can't see," he said. "And I feel very sorry for you because, bro, that woman is drop-dead gorgeous."

"Pretty like how?" Zac needed a mental picture.

"Not pretty. Way past that. Stunning is a good word. Like a movie star." Drew shifted, his boots thudding against the floor. "I doubt I'll do Abby justice, but I'll try. She's shorter than us, but taller than Mandy. Her hair is sort of fluffy, loose curls, maybe."

"How long?" Zac asked.

"Four or five inches past her shoulders. It's black, or almost, and very shiny against her pale skin. She doesn't have much of a tan, but she's got these amazing eyes."

"Amazing eyes?" Zac made a face. "How can eyes be amazing?"

"Well—hmm." Drew stopped to think about it. "Like kind of changing all the time. At first I thought they were green, but then I noticed they change depending on what she's wearing or maybe her mood. Sometimes they look the color of glacial meltwater. With a turquoise tinge? I don't know to explain it. Abby's different."

"Her face?" Zac was building an image in his mind and he wanted details.

"I told you. She's beautiful. But it's funny." Drew huffed slightly as he straightened. "After you get over her stunning beauty, you realize that's not what makes Abby so amazing. It's a kind of glow when she smiles that makes you pay attention. Mandy's noticed it, too. Radiating loveliness, she calls it."

"You're not much help," Zac complained. "You make her sound like some kind of fairy-tale character."

"Actually, she reminds me a bit of a character

in one of Ella's DVDs. You'll understand when you see her for yourself," Drew promised as he grabbed his arm. "Ready to go?"

"Yes. You can let go of my arm, bro. I know my way off the deck." Zac grabbed the handrail and stepped down, silently counting as he went. Because he'd heard Drew drive up, he had a fair idea where the car was parked. He found the door handle and got in.

"Can we go now?" Ella demanded. "I want to play the peanut game."

"What's a peanut game?" Zoe demanded.

"Ah, you have no idea, girls. Let the fun begin," Drew cheered as he drove away.

And it was fun, even though Zac couldn't see. He could hear the girls as they laughed and giggled and tried to keep him informed about what they were doing. Abby did, too, but Zac refused to let her stay at his side the entire time.

"There's usually a game like golf. It has the best prizes, if memory serves," he told her. "See it?"

"I don't see it, but there is one where you toss plastic discs in a cup. I'll try that." Abby returned from the game a few minutes later, elated at having won a hand-beaded leather coin purse made by a local Blackfoot woman.

"It's so well constructed," she marveled, insisting he feel her treasure. "Aren't you going to participate in anything?" When he shook his head, she called Drew over. "Zac won't try any games."

"Can't have that." Drew grabbed his brother's arm and pulled him upright. "I'm pretty sure you can't best me at the dart game, but you have to try."

"Dude, I can't see," Zac reminded him, annoyed by his brother's pushiness.

"Neither will anyone else. Because we do this blindfolded, remember?"

Zac had forgotten. Actually, he'd forgotten a lot about these fun evenings and how Miss P. always planned for total participation. Young, old, infirm, physically and mentally challenged and those who just needed to be around others all had a place in her scheme. He'd play this game because, if he didn't, she'd seek him out and make a scene.

Abby wove her arm in his as she directed him to the game and told him it was set up in a protected space where children weren't allowed.

"Okay. Here's the dart." Drew pushed Zac's fingertips over the Velcro tip. "Feel it? Good," he said when Zac nodded. "Now the target is about two feet around and it's straight in front of you, maybe ten feet away."

"Maybe? I need a more accurate description than that," Zac protested.

"It's actually ten and three-quarters feet from the line on the floor. Your toes are just touch-

ing that line," Miss Partridge advised from behind him.

How did the woman know the exact moment
to appear?

"What will I win?" he asked as he hefted the
extralong dart several times to test its weight.

"That's a surprise." Miss Partridge laughed
with great glee, which made Zac extremely sus-
picious. "Go ahead now, dear. This is a popular
event and we have lots of folks getting in line."

"The pressure mounts," Drew murmured. The
smile in his voice indicated he was teasing.

"Ignore them, Zac. You can do this. Piece of
cake." Abby's whisper came from the direction
of his left ear. "You'll have to throw with some
force because the board isn't very stable and several folks have had their darts fall off. Oh, and
aim just slightly left. There's an overhead fan that
seems to be skewing things a bit."

"Thanks," he said. Odd how her simple instructions and reassurance settled his uneasiness.
"Here goes nothing."

Zac exhaled, shut out the noise around him and
concentrated on exactly where he wanted the dart
to go. Then he tossed it and heard the resulting
thud. At least the dart had stuck. He hoped. He
waited for his result. But nobody said anything,
which was extremely disconcerting.

"Abby? Did I completely miss?" Zac twisted

his head from side to side, trying to catch a whiff of her fragrance so he could figure out where she stood. She didn't respond. "Is something wrong?"

"Not unless you don't like a perfect bull's-eye," Drew said with a groan. "How am I supposed to beat that?"

"You can't." Zac smirked, satisfaction swelling inside. "You never could, as I recall."

"Don't look too smug, bro. It's the best two out of three," Drew informed him haughtily.

But as it turned out, Zac hit the bull's-eye two out of three times and ended up with the highest score. Miss P. took great delight in awarding his prize of a free dinner for two at a local upscale restaurant.

"You and Abby will enjoy a nice meal together," she told him with obvious delight. "Alone."

Zac felt Abby stiffen beside him. If he could, he would have glared at the former librarian. Instead he thanked her, then asked, "Where are the girls, Abby?"

"Fishing." Was that relief in his nurse's voice? If so it quickly disappeared. "Mandy's with them and they're having a ball."

"Good. So there's time for you to try something else. Name your choice." He was ready for her protest, but Abby surprised him.

"I found your putting green. It's set up on the front lawn outside." Zac doubted she realized how wistful she sounded. "I've always had a yen to play golf. Do you think I can try that?"

"Why not? Though it's probably going to be difficult to play in the dark." With her arm under his hand he walked out with her. "Like playing blind," he groused.

"It's not really dark. Anyway, the streetlight is right above us. Quite convenient." She paused. "Will you be all right waiting here?"

"Of course. Now go sink that ball." He inhaled the nuances of her fragrance, even more attractive in the evening air.

"I hope I don't make an idiot of myself," he heard her murmur as she removed her arm. "Here goes."

Abby tried to sink the ball several times and was exceptionally unsuccessful at it, judging by her play-by-play description.

"Well," she huffed when she rejoined him. "I just saved myself a lot of money."

"Really?" At her side, Zac returned to the hall. "How?"

"By not investing in golf clubs or the rest of the gear that goes with them. Clearly golf is not my forte." Her good-natured laugh said she wasn't bothered by that one bit.

Zac couldn't help smiling, too. It felt good to forget his worries and relax, even if only for a little while.

"Daddy! Daddy!"

And like that he tensed.

"What's wrong?" he demanded as Mia's and Zoe's hands laced through his, one on each side.

"We're hungry, Daddy."

"Oh. Well, that's easily remedied. Miss Partridge always makes sure there's a ton of food at these things." He shifted, suddenly aware of Abby's absence. Funny how vulnerable he felt without her calming presence.

"I'm here," she said as if reading his thoughts. "There's an area to the left where you could sit while I help the girls choose a snack."

"I want something to munch on, too," he said, feeling himself relax again.

"Okay. I'll get you—"

"Chocolate cake," Zac finished for her, and grinned. "Miss P. always brings a chocolate cake to these things. It will have four layers of white icing with some kind of berries on top. I can't tell you how many times I fell asleep in Africa dreaming about that cake."

"I'll look for it." Humor laced Abby's response. "Coffee, too? With cream?"

"Yes, please. And thank you." It was foolish to feel like an invalid, and yet that was how Zac felt as Abby helped him find a seat at a long table before promising to return with the girls shortly.

Those not involved in a game or conversation stopped by to chat with him. The pastor wanted to know if he was interested in speaking at an upcoming men's meeting, which Zac declined with a nonchalant, "Later, perhaps." Even Leo sought him out to comment on his dart-throwing prowess in his slow methodical drawl. Then Zac asked if Leo had won at anything.

"Nah. But doesn't matter. Great times, these events," Leo mumbled. "Don't see our neighbors often enough."

Zac agreed, frowning as he heard Leo shuffle away. The man still seemed despondent. Were their talks doing any good?

"There were three chocolate cakes," Abby announced as something brushed his hand. "I brought a piece of each even though everyone is staring at me for my gluttony." She sounded amused. "Mia will sit beside you while I go back and help Zoe. Coffee is on your right."

"Did Abby get anything for herself to eat?" Zac asked his daughter in an undertone when Abby had left.

"No. But maybe she will." Mia pressed something to his lips. "Taste, Daddy. It's so good."

"Yes, it is, honey." Zac bit into a peanut-butter-covered dill pickle and strove not to make a face. He declined a second helping and sipped his coffee to rinse away the taste as he listened to the hubbub around him. He could hear Mandy and Drew teasing Abby as they and Zoe drew near.

"That's how you stay so slender?" Mandy asked, sounding slightly disgusted. "By eating pie?"

"I like pie." Abby sounded defensive. She brushed Zac's arm as she sat next to him. "Besides, someone said there's line dancing later. I'll get my exercise then, though I'm not really sure what it is. Dancing in a line?"

Zac hoped she didn't expect him to make a fool of himself dancing. Ordinarily he'd have gladly taken the floor with her, but with no eyesight he'd be a stumbling, bumbling fool.

"Are we gonna dance, Daddy?" Zoe asked, her mouth full.

"The music's starting," Mia added.

"Uh, I—" Zac scrambled for an excuse.

"Let's enjoy our snack before we decide," Abby interceded calmly. "Chicken salad sandwiches are my favorite. After lemon pie."

When the kids' voices offered cover, Zac leaned near Abby.

"Thanks for getting me out of that," he murmured.

"Oh, you're not out of anything," she said, that ever-present smile in her voice. "You did say I'm in Montana now, and I understand that line dancing is a must for everyone here. So you're going to teach me. Eat up, cowboy."

Something in her tone told him she wasn't joking.

Zac ate his favorite chocolate cake without tasting a bite.

Chapter Six

Abby knew Zac was dreading it, but she felt certain that getting out on the dance floor with everyone else would help ease him out of his self-imposed isolation.

At least, she hoped so.

While he lingered over his coffee, she studied the dancers' movements. It didn't look terribly difficult, but then everyone seemed to know exactly which way to turn and move. Almost of their own volition, her toes began to mimic their steps.

"You're going to insist I get up there and make an idiot of myself, aren't you?" Zac sounded grumpy.

"Uh-huh. Just like the rest of us, Doc." She grabbed his hand. "Come on. I want to try. It will be easy for you because you've probably line-danced a hundred times before."

"Never blind," he assured her dryly.

"First time for both of us, then." Abby couldn't explain why she was so excited when the music stopped and folks waited for the next tune from the band on the stage. As they walked toward the dance floor, Zac's arm brushed hers, sending a shiver rippling through her. Silly, perhaps, but it felt as if they were building some deeper connection. "Explain line dancing to me, please?"

"You've been watching." Zac shrugged. "And I heard your toes tapping. Line dancing is just people standing in lines, doing the same steps together. Follow everyone else and you'll get it."

"Not much help, are you?" She reached for his hand, thinking she'd guide him. Zac started laughing. "What?"

"No touching in line dancing, at least not as we do it here. You'll just have to endure me stomping on your toes. When I do, remember that you're the one who insisted I do this." He snickered when she jerked her hand away. Her breath caught at his relaxed expression. He looked exactly like the cowboy she'd seen in a magazine at the library. "Watch Mandy," he advised. "Follow her lead."

Actually, Abby found it much easier to watch Zac. For someone who couldn't see, he was incredibly light on his feet and seemed to know every move in advance. She felt bad about repeatedly bumping into him, but since other newbies looked just as awkward, she relaxed and allowed herself to enjoy this new experience.

"I've got to take a break," she said after they'd finished the third and most intricate dance yet. "Zoe is watching us. Want to dance with her?"

"Why not? I've already embarrassed myself." That wry curve of his lips was firmly back in place.

"It's me who's embarrassing herself. You're not even winded," Abby noted in disgust. Funny thing was, she didn't care. Ken wasn't here to mock her or remind her of all the reasons she needed to be circumspect. Here, in this place, nobody was making fun of anyone. Everyone was just enjoying themselves. She was, too.

She waved Zoe over and left father and daughter together while she and Mia found cool drinks and a place to sit. Mia proudly displayed the prizes she'd won at the ring toss and the egg race.

"Wow. You did really well." Surprised Mia wasn't clamoring to take Zoe's place she asked, "Are you going to dance with your dad after Zoe?"

"Nope," the little girl said, ducking her head into her chest.

"Why not, sweetie?"

"'Cause I don't know how." Mia fiddled with her glass, a frown marring her pretty face.

"Sweetie, I didn't know how, either. Neither does Zoe. But we learned. A little bit," she said, remembering her stumbles. "Nobody cares how well you dance. Everyone's here to have fun and enjoy themselves."

"Ella cares. She said she knows all the dances." Mia's bottom lip thrust out in a pout. "She knows all kind of stuff."

"Does she?" Something was going on. Abby had to find out what it was. "What does Ella know?"

"She knows how to ride a bike. An' she knows about stars and the moon. She knows all the kids who are here. Her mommy and daddy teach her lotsa stuff." Mia exhaled and then blurted, "Uncle Drew even teached her how to ride horses. Why doesn't my daddy teach me an' Zoe how to ride horses?"

"Did you ask him?" Abby asked.

"Yeah." Mia's sad eyes met hers. "But Daddy doesn't like it when me and Zoe ask him about riding Grandpa's horses. He gets a mad face an' says we aren't big enough yet. But we are!"

"Well, honey, I think you *are* big enough to understand something about your daddy." Abby swallowed as she searched for the right words, because, despite her belief that the twins were more than capable of learning to ride, she needed Mia to understand Zac's perspective. "Daddies are very careful about the people they love. Your daddy really loves you and Zoe so he worries about you both. Because your daddy can't see right now, he worries extra."

"But—"

"Just listen for a minute, Mia." Abby saw Zac's smile flash as he taught Zoe the steps. She prayed desperately for a way to help this sweet girl comprehend her father's struggles. An idea took shape. She quickly stowed their used drinking glasses in the wash-up bin and then grasped Mia's hand. "Come with me."

"Where are we going?" Mia wondered as she followed.

"Here. This is perfect." Abby chose a vacant spot behind the hall where a wall sconce lit up the area. Then she removed her scarf.

"What are we gonna do?" Mia wondered with a frown in her voice.

"I want to show you something." She wound the scarf around Mia's eyes and tied it in the back. "Now, what can you see?"

"Nothing!" Mia said, obviously disgruntled. "'Cause you tied your scarf an'—"

"That's right. Now listen. Hear the music that's playing inside? See if you can dance to it."

Mia tried to shuffle in the longish grass and stumbled. "I can't do it," she said indignantly.

"Well, can you walk toward me?" Again Mia

faltered. Abby grasped her arm. "It's not easy, is it? But your dad is dancing and, for him, it's just the same as if he has a scarf over his eyes."

"Yeah, I guess. But Uncle Drew could teach us how to ride a horse," Mia objected as she pulled off the scarf. "He teached Ella."

"You know, I think it was Ella's mom who taught her to ride, but that's not the point." Abby retied the chiffon around her neck before squatting in front of the little girl. "The thing is, Mia, your dad can't just take off his eye coverings whenever he gets tired of them."

"I know." Mia's shoulders drooped with disappointment.

"I'm sure it's very hard for your daddy to wait until the doctor says it's okay to uncover his eyes." She searched for a way to help this child understand the pressure Zac withstood every day. "It's not because he doesn't want them off. It's not because he doesn't want you and Zoe to ride the horses. He does. He wants so badly to see and enjoy all the things you do. He also wants to make sure you girls are all right. So he waits, just like the doctor says, even though it's difficult for him."

"'Cause Daddy's patient?" Mia said thoughtfully.

"Yes, and you and Zoe must be patient, too," she coaxed. "You *will* learn to ride, Mia, but for now you have to wait. You can do that, can't you? Because we don't want your daddy to uncover his eyes too early."

"No." The little girl frowned. "'Cause if he does, then he might not never see us."

"Right. So no more asking about riding horses for a while?" Abby asked, hoping the little girl had understood.

"Nope," Mia agreed. "'Cause he's my daddy an' I love him, an' we're not s'posed to make people that love us be worried." She paused, frowned. "I want Daddy to laugh and be happy, like he usta before we comed to Grandma and Grandpa's."

"He will be, sweetie. I'm sure he will. We'll pray for that every day." Abby hugged this darling child, her heart swelling with love.

They returned inside where Mia changed places with Zoe, who left to try another round of the fishing game, hoping to best her sister. With a tart from the dessert table in one hand and a cup of tea in the other, Abby chose an out-of-the-way corner to watch Zac, wishing she had the courage to dance with him again.

"So Zac doesn't want to let the children learn to ride, hmm?" Miss Partridge's question broke Abby's reverie.

"Um." Since she wasn't sure how much to reveal, Abby ignored the question. "Join me," she added, since the lady also carried a steaming cup and a sweet treat.

"Thank you, dear, I will." Once seated, the former librarian leaned nearer to murmur, "Please forgive me, but I was outside taking a breath of fresh air and I couldn't help overhearing you and Mia. You handled her issues quite wonderfully."

"Thank you, but it's only a temporary fix." Abby tasted her blueberry tart as she considered the issue of riding. "The girls have asked about it before and they will ask again. It's totally normal that they should want to ride since they're so close in age to Ella and she rides almost every day. But Zac just isn't ready for them to do it."

"I suppose he feels he's missing special moments in his kids' lives." Miss Partridge frowned. "You know, it seems to me as if he's cutting himself off at the Double H."

Having heard Drew and Zac mention Miss Partridge's penchant for gossip, Abby was immediately wary.

"It's difficult for him to get around since he can't see," she said in his defense.

"I suppose. That's why I thought he and Leo both might benefit from their meetings. But maybe it isn't right for them. I'll have to pray about it some more." Miss Partridge was silent for several moments before suddenly blurting,

"Would you like to meet for coffee sometime, Abby? Just to talk?"

"That would be fun." The notion that Miss Partridge might be lonely grew. It was silly. The lady knew everyone, had lived in Sunshine for years and could visit to her heart's content. And yet, out of all her acquaintances, she'd chosen Abby. "Except, I don't know when I'd be free to come into town."

"That's okay." The elderly librarian smiled eagerly. "I could come to you. Maybe we could even take the twins for a walk or a picnic if Zac needs the house."

"I'm sure the girls would love that," Abby said.

Zac and Zoe had finished dancing, but since Mandy was now drawing them toward a group of what seemed to be old friends, Abby felt no compunction about continuing her visit with Miss Partridge. This woman deeply interested her.

"I love your hair," she said, obeying an inner nudge to offer encouragement. "You should never cover it. That tone of silvery gray emphasizes the blue in your eyes."

"Why, thank you, dear." For a moment Miss Partridge looked totally nonplussed. She blinked as she lifted one hand and touched the few strands that had worked free of her cloche hat. "It's hard to control with all these curls so I usually keep it under wraps."

"You know, that's what our first date should be about," Abby said as ideas grew. "We should have a beauty date. We can share ideas."

"Really?" The librarian's blue eyes sparkled like a young girl's. "I've never done that. It would be so wonderful. Are you sure?"

"Positive. I was at the store with Mandy the other day and I bought a play makeup set thinking I'd give it to the girls on a rainy day, but they could be part of our beauty day. They'd love it." She was delighted by the prospect of really getting to know this lady. "Which day works best for you?"

They had almost settled on a date when Abby heard Zac say her name.

"Over here," she called, alert for any stumble as the doctor felt his way around the tables, following her voice. "Miss Partridge and I are planning a beauty afternoon and we were wondering when your, um, client's next appointment is." Her heart immediately picked up its pace while her eyes admired him.

His jeans were perfect for this evening, comfortable looking with naturally worn areas on the knees. His scuffed black boots seemed to scream *cowboy*, a look much enhanced by the way his hair drooped over one eyebrow in a carless curve. Except for his eye coverings, Zac Calhoun was a picture-perfect testament to ranch living.

"We're getting together the day after tomorrow. After lunch." He felt his way over to them and asked with more than a hint of surprise, "What is a beauty afternoon?"

"It's just for us girls," Miss Partridge said with a hint of coquettishness. "Sorry, Zac. No men. Now I'd better get back to my duties. See you then, Abby."

"Yes. It will be fun." Abby watched her walk away, then chuckled at the downward tilt of Zac's lips. "She's gone, so you can say what you're so obviously thinking."

"The mind boggles with my thoughts," he said cynically. "A beauty afternoon with the town's former librarian, who, by the way, has to be eons older than you, will be fun?"

"Hardly eons. And it will be. Miss Partridge is smart and witty and knows everyone so she's a wealth of information." Abby shrugged. "She's been a great help getting you all that psychology stuff you wanted, hasn't she?" He nodded. "Besides, I think she's lonely. Why shouldn't I spend some time with her?"

"No reason at all, if you want to," he agreed as his forehead furrowed. "Perhaps you're lonely, too? I should have realized."

"I'm not lonely," she denied. "But I'm very curious about Sunshine and its people, so visiting with her will be great. Also, I really like Miss P."

"Okay," he said blankly, as if she wasn't making sense. "That's good. I guess." Suddenly his lips curved down in a frown. "I can't hear the girls."

"That's because they're stuffing their mouths with popcorn while they watch the puppet show, which we missed because you were grilling me about Miss Partridge. They're fine." She thought Zac seemed somewhat frustrated. "Did you want to leave now?"

"No, let them enjoy the show. We'll leave when it's finished." He felt for the chair, then sat down beside her. "Between watching the twins and me, did you get to participate in anything but a couple of dances?"

"I had a great time." Why did she still feel that little glow from dancing when they had barely touched hands? *Get over yourself,* she ordered her brain. "Miss Partridge has gone to an extensive amount of work to make tonight so much fun."

"Yes," he admitted. "Of course, there are always lots of volunteers."

"Zac," she said in a chastising voice. "To spearhead something like this isn't easy no matter how much help you have." Abby glanced around. "Everyone is engaged. That's a real testament to her thoughtfulness about every person who attended." She hesitated before deciding to go for broke. "It seems like you have some kind of grudge against Miss Partridge."

"I do," he said harshly. "She spread untruths about my parents."

"Purposely?" Taken aback by the confession, Abby waited for an explanation.

Several minutes passed before Zac heaved a sigh and shook his head.

"You know what? It was a long time ago and I don't want to rehash it all over again. Anyway, my mom forgave her so I should, too."

"It still rankles, though. Right?" Abby smiled at his nod. "Forgiveness is hard. It costs to forgive and sometimes it seems like the other person doesn't deserve it."

"How did you get so smart?" He didn't wait for her answer. "You probably think someone who's been a missionary should have forgiven Miss P. long ago."

"Why would I think that? You're human, aren't you?" Abby cupped her hands around her tea. "I have a few of my own forgiveness issues to work on," she admitted very quietly. "Sometimes I think I've dealt with it all and then smack! I'm back to square one, repeating my prayers, asking God to heal my heart again so I can release my pain."

"Someone must have done a number on you," he murmured. "I've never heard you speak ill of anyone, and yet, just now there was a note in your voice—anger, maybe? Or, no, hurt that you're trying to hide. Who hurt you, Abby?"

Though she knew Zac could not see her, Abby felt as if he was probing her soul. Why hadn't she shut up, made light of her past? Why had she let him see…?

"I think it was Ken." Zac's quiet assertion shocked her.

"How did you—?" She caught herself from finishing that sentence. "You don't have to counsel me," she said firmly.

"I wouldn't dream of it." He folded his hands on the table. "When I first met you, I sensed this reserve about you, as if you were protecting yourself. Not with the twins. You're always open and honest with them. But there was something else."

"You were under a strain," she excused him. "You probably imagined that."

"I don't think so." A funny smile twisted his lips. "When Drew met you, there was a funny catch to his voice that I couldn't understand so a while ago I asked him about it."

"Oh." Did she really want to hear this?

"He said you're stunningly beautiful."

"That was nice of him, though it's not true." She was glad he couldn't see her blush.

"Drew wouldn't lie to me." Zac sounded certain. "What he said, or maybe the way he said it, confirmed my impression that you are reserved around adults. But you've formed a strong liking for Miss Partridge, so I assume it's men that bother you."

"I don't want to talk—" she protested, but Zac interrupted her.

"My evidence is that when you change my dressings, you catch your breath, maybe so you can force yourself to touch me. But I would never hurt you, Abby," he said very gently. "Never."

"I never thought you would." Shocked that he'd assumed the worst, she wanted to deny his conclusions. And yet, she couldn't because they were at least partly true. "It's not you, Zac. It's that sometimes certain things from the past kind of overwhelm me, make me forget it's over now and—oh, never mind." *Stop talking, Abby!*

"But I do mind." Zac's hand brushed hers. She could smell his aftershave as he leaned toward her. "Please talk to me. I don't think you've shared this with anyone and you need to. Otherwise your past will keep returning to bother you."

It was so tempting. Abby opened her mouth to tell him, but was interrupted.

"Can we go home, Daddy?" Zoe yawned. "I'm tired."

"Maybe another time, Zac. But thank you for understanding." Abby rose and glanced around to find her other charge. "I'll get Mia and then we can leave," she said quickly, and rushed away before he could stop her.

Zac was right. She did feel like she needed to talk to someone, to let out the pain and remorse and sadness that kept building inside. But not to Zac.

She was already nervous of the unusual feelings that mushroomed inside whenever he was near. Telling him her horrible past, opening herself up to let him hear all the ugliness—no! And why not?

Because, Abby realized, she didn't want this man for whom she was growing increasingly fond, to think less of her or feel sorry for her. She'd just have to rely more heavily on God for courage.

Chapter Seven

❦

"You gotta come, Daddy," Zoe insisted. "Abby's got a s'prise."

"Yeah, a s'prise," Mia echoed, dragging at his arm. "We like s'prises."

"What's going on, Abby?" She'd been away all afternoon, and only now that they'd finished clearing up from supper did it occur to Zac to wonder why.

The past week had been filled with challenges, including a bout of flu, which had kept the girls housebound and left him scrambling for a quiet place to talk to Leo. Then Abby's beauty time with Miss Partridge the other day had turned the little log house into a kind of salon, which meant Zac's only refuge was the deck. But even there he found no peace in listening to an audiobook. Boisterous laughter had made him feel left out.

"I can't tell you my surprise. I have to show

you." She stopped, cleared her throat. "Uh, I mean, you need to see something." There was that smile again, weaving its way through her words. "Oh, stop standing there and come along," she ordered, and punctuated that with a laugh. "It won't hurt you."

"Where are we going?" He hung up the dish-towel.

"You'll see. Oh." Her quiet gasp at the faux pas made him smile. "I mean—"

"Let's go." He swept his hand in front of him. "Ready, girls?"

The twins jabbered and skipped and hopped their way out. Zac followed, negotiating the stairs easily. At the bottom he waited for new directions. Abby took his hand.

"Do you mind? It's a little uneven where we're going."

That made him nervous, but he walked beside her as best he could, his hand in her warm one while his curiosity grew. As they walked, he got his bearings.

"We're going to Peace Meadow," he guessed.

Abby didn't respond because just then the rest of his family joined them.

"What's going on?" Ben wanted to know.

"You'll see," Mandy said. Meaning she was in on this surprise, too?

Zac had little time to puzzle it out. Walking

over the uneven ground took all his concentration. He was grateful for Abby's steady grip.

"Oh, my!" Bonnie's gasp startled Zac as much as Abby's sudden tug on his hand to stop him from moving forward.

"Abby, this is way beyond what we discussed." Mandy sounded shocked.

"It's fantastic." Drew grabbed his brother's arm. "Four, maybe five steps more."

Zac complied, taken aback when his leg bumped into something. He leaned down.

"A chair?" he asked.

"Ten of them," Drew corrected. "Brilliant red. Some kind of manmade material?" he guessed.

"Never needs paint and can withstand weather," Mandy explained, her voice light with a hint of laughter. "Abby and I saw them at the hardware store and thought they'd be perfect here. What she has created—" She paused, then said in an awestruck voice, "This is way beyond perfect."

"What are you talking about?" Zac demanded in frustration.

"Son, the ladies have done an amazing job of turning Peace Meadow into, well, I don't know exactly what to call it." Ben's awe-filled voice showed how moved he was. "The red chairs are grouped around a huge firepit."

"Me an' Mia an' Ella got our own chairs, Daddy. Yellow ones," Zoe explained excitedly.

"There's a gazebo?" Bonnie gaped. "How did you know I've always wished we had a gazebo here?"

"You mentioned that and I thought it sounded perfect so why not?" Abby's soft voice oozed satisfaction. "This particular gazebo has screens that can be let down if the bugs come out. It will provide shade from the hot sun and shelter from rain."

"How did you do all this by yourself, Abby?" Mandy demanded.

"The hardware store set up everything. I just told them where to put it." As usual, Abby brushed off their words of praise. "Your family gives and gives to everyone who comes to the ranch. I thought it was time you all had a place to be together or by yourselves, to relax without strangers to entertain."

"It's amazing, dear. How thoughtful of you. It really is *Peace* Meadow now." Zac thought his mom was probably hugging Abby.

"There's a picnic table, Zac," Drew told him. "With a huge umbrella. And food."

"You would notice that part." Mandy laughed. "Abby, that little shelter is a perfect solution for keeping the firewood dry."

"Putting those hooks on the end means we can leave s'more forks here and not have to carry them back and forth." Ben sounded happy. "Abby, you've made Peace Meadow absolutely perfect. We haven't used it much lately, I'm sorry to say. But now we can come here together or separately, have fun, read or just sit a spell and think."

"Hey! There's toys in this box," Ella squealed.

Zac kept absorbing information, trying to visualize the scene in his mind.

"I hope you'll all use it for years to come," Abby murmured.

"Let's enjoy it now. Drew, can you build a fire?" Mandy asked. "Girls, let's get our s'mores ready."

"It's really lovely, dear. So thoughtful of you to include a gazebo." His mom sounded tearful. "Thank you for pulling this all together. I'm going to love reading my Bible out here on summer mornings."

"You're most welcome," Abby said.

Zac figured they were hugging again. He felt his way into a chair and found it very comfortable. While the others examined every detail and oohed over the weatherproof chests that held an assortment of items to make the area self-sufficient, his mental picture grew. Now if only he could actually see what Abby looked like.

"Are you all right?" she asked quietly as she pressed a soda can into his hand, her fingers warm against his.

"I'm fine. I was just wishing I could see it all."

He tilted his head to one side. "It sounds like a pretty big undertaking. Why would you go to all this trouble for people you hardly know, Abby?"

"I feel like I do know your family," she responded after a slight pause that made him wince at the note of hurt in her words.

"Hey, I didn't mean it like that. Of course you know us. It's just that—" He stopped and tried to figure out how to explain himself.

"You think it was too much. That I shouldn't have done it." Her hand dropped away from his, leaving a chill. "I'm sorry. I thought—never mind."

"No, Abby, I…" He realized she'd moved away. Frustrated that he'd made her feel bad for doing something so nice, his fingers tightened around the pop can.

"Better relax that grip or you'll be wearing the stuff," Mandy advised, her voice harsh. "Not that I wouldn't like to dump it over you myself. How could you hurt Abby like that, Zac? Don't you understand how much joy she found in doing this for us? For you?"

"I didn't mean—for me?" He started in confusion.

"When we first saw the chairs in the store, she was so excited. She said we always share the ranch with everyone. She said the meadow should be our private place where no one but the

family came. A place to get away, to reconnect."
Mandy's tone softened. "She wanted to pay for
it all herself but I insisted the ranch could afford
a few chairs and a picnic table."

"Sounds like this is more than that," he muttered, abashed that he'd said anything.

"Way more. Because Abby doesn't just talk to
folks, she listens. She knew your mom's always
wanted a gazebo, that your dad likes to sit outside and watch his birds. She knows Drew's crazy
about building campfires and that the kids would
love running wild and free out here." Mandy's
voice softened. "Most of all, she thought about
you."

"But I don't—" He didn't get to finish.

Mandy's voice dropped. "The bills I paid didn't
include any of the special things that make this
such a fantastic refuge. Not toys, not the gazebo,
not the firewood box or—"

"Meaning Abby paid for the extras herself?
But why would she go to such trouble, and expense?" Zac couldn't figure that out.

"Because that's who Abby is," Mandy insisted.
"She tries to make life better for everyone."

"But this sounds like a lot of extras!" he argued.

"Yes. They're thoughtful additions that make
Peace Meadow usable by all of us. You're around
Abby every day, Zac. She treats your eyes, looks

after your daughters, keeps your home running smoothly and probably does a host of other things, most of which aren't in her job description," Mandy reminded him.

"That's true." Abby did an awful lot for him and the girls.

"And she enjoys every moment of it. Don't you understand her yet?" his sister-in-law scolded. "Abby acts from the heart. She's a giver. In fixing up Peace Meadow she thought about you, too."

"About me?" He was confused by that.

"Especially you. She knows how difficult it is for you to talk to Leo when the kids are running in and out of the house. She thought having a serene place like this to come to, where you could be alone without interruption, would offer privacy and solace for both of you." Mandy sighed. "Open your eyes, brother dear. Figuratively, I mean. Abby cares about people. She cares about you."

Abby cared about him? The thought made Zac nervous. He wasn't interested in another relationship. Was he? He would have pressed Mandy for details, but he heard the swish of her footsteps moving through the grass, away from him. As irritated as she'd sounded, she probably wouldn't tell him more, anyway.

Zac sat absorbing the sound of his family's laughter, listening as Ben jokingly critiqued

Drew's fire-building expertise, as Mandy taste-tested and exclaimed over the snacks Abby had provided, as his mom taught the kids how to play croquet. Everyone was enjoying the evening. But where was Abby?

"I'm going to try making a s'more." She spoke from directly in front of him. "Would you like one? I should warn you that I've never made one before."

"Does Drew have the fire going?" When she said yes, Zac shook his head. "Better wait until the flames die a bit. Otherwise the marshmallow will light and you'll get charcoal." He frowned. "You've really never made a s'more before?"

"It wasn't something we did," she said simply. A little puff of air told him she'd taken the chair next to his.

"We did. A lot." He tilted his head back and let the plethora of smells assail his senses. "I've been sitting here remembering the fun times we always had on the Double H. We boys were very blessed to be adopted by Ben and Bonnie. And now this family is blessed again. Because of you. Thank you, Abby."

"Oh." He felt her stare. "Well, you're welcome." Then after a short pause, she murmured, "I thought you didn't like it."

"I never said that," he protested. "It sounds wonderful. I'm sure we'll all enjoy it for years to come. But—Mandy said you didn't charge it all to the ranch. This…" He waved a hand to indicate what she'd done. "It had to be expensive," he added hesitantly.

"Is that what bothers you? The money?" Abby laughed, but oddly, Zac didn't hear much mirth in it. "Don't worry, I have plenty of money."

"It's really none of my business." He felt stupid for probing. "It's just—with traveling all this way and the airline upgrades you paid for us and everything else…" He mentioned it deliberately, certain now that she'd been the benefactor of their first-class seats. "I don't want you to find yourself short."

"I won't be short of money, Zac." Abby's cool voice told him she was annoyed. She probably thought he was prying into her personal affairs.

Her next words startled him.

"I have more money than I'll ever use, thanks to an insurance settlement from my parents' deaths." The brusque tone was so unlike Abby.

"I'm sorry," he said quickly. "You don't have to explain to me."

"I do if it will help you understand why I did this." She heaved a gigantic sigh. "My parents died because of a very powerful, very drunk politician who wanted to avoid publicity and a charge for wrongful death. It's a lot of money, hush money, which I will not use for myself. In addition, I also received insurance money from Ken's and Levi's deaths."

"So in both instances, the arrival of the money coincided with great loss," he said, beginning to understand. "Abby, I'm sorry."

"My parents, Levi—" She stopped, swallowed hard, then continued in an almost inaudible whisper. "That money can never make up for the people I've lost."

"Of course not." Zac still didn't comprehend why she'd felt compelled to fix up Peace Meadow, but he knew he needed to listen. "Nobody would think money could compensate for such loss."

"Ken did." Abby's murmur shocked him but he kept quiet, suddenly certain that she needed to say this. "He was always after me to buy this or that. 'Make our lives easier,' he'd say. 'Your parents would want that.'"

"You don't think they would have?" Zac leaned back in his chair, relieved his family was busy with the fire allowing the two of them privacy to talk.

"My parents wanted me to be happy, yes," she responded. "But they knew the true source of happiness. They knew real joy doesn't come from things. It comes from giving."

"So you feel you should use the money to make others happy," he guessed.

"Not exactly." Abby sighed. "It's more that

I've been entrusted, that it's my duty to see that the money is used to bless and help others. My parents devoted their lives to people. That's why they left their home and moved to Africa. Giving what they had meant more to them than gaining dollars." She gave a funny little laugh. "Do I sound smug and self-righteous? That's what Ken always said."

"Ken didn't get it," Zac told her without hesitation. "I do. You want to use your inheritance in a way that honors your parents, who deserve to be honored. And I'm honored that you chose to share it with my family. Thank you."

"Does that mean you'll use Peace Meadow?" she asked, sounding puzzled.

Zac had a hunch that if he said yes, he'd be opening the door to something he couldn't control. So he stayed silent.

But how he wished he felt confident in God's renewal of his sight, that he felt assured he even had a future in which he could promise Abby he'd make use of her generous gesture.

Abby felt Zac's hesitation in his silence. She wasn't offended by it. He would need time to adapt to the changes this space offered. She would encourage him in every step.

"Where are the twins?" Zac asked.

"Waiting for the fire to burn down. Like you,

Drew insists they don't begin roasting their marshmallows until it does." She had to smile at the girls' dancing feet. They, like most kids, couldn't stay still for long. "Your brother's holding Mandy's hand, just like your dad's holding your mom's. Your family is so cute."

"They love each other, that's for sure." Zac turned his head toward her and asked cautiously, "Do you mind if I ask you a couple more questions about your inheritance?"

"Not much more to tell." She so didn't want to think about her pain and loss anymore. Why had she ever mentioned it to him? "What would you like to know?"

"Why are you so determined that your money must go to enriching others' lives? Why isn't it okay to spend some on yourself, to make *your* life easier?" He stopped, then blurted in a rush, "Would it have been so terrible to buy your husband that airplane he wanted?"

Abby winced. His question echoed Ken's. And what really hurt was that underlying Zac's words lay a criticism that cut more deeply than Ken's ever had.

"I'm sorry," he apologized quickly. "I shouldn't have said that."

"It's been said before." She gathered her composure. "Ken was very angry with me for refusing, especially the last time he asked. I have this feeling that he was trying to show off his skill, to prove he was above such a *simple* plane, as he called it. I believe that's why he insisted Levi and I go with him on his last flight."

There—she'd said it. She exhaled, relieved when Zac didn't tell her she was being foolish.

"And you feel guilty for refusing him," he said softly. "You believe you caused him to crash because he was so intent on showing off for you. Am I close?"

"You've verbalized it better than I could." She accepted his judgment. She'd accepted her part in her family's deaths long ago. "I made the money too important," she murmured. "There was plenty. Ken could have had a newer plane without even making a dent in the insurance."

"But you wouldn't buy it because...?" He tilted his head to one side, waiting for her to finish.

"Because it was such a frivolous expenditure. Because it was like devaluing my parents' lives." She squeezed her eyes against the tears that threatened. "Because the only way I could accept that money was to see it as their gift to me. Otherwise accepting it was simply greed, like I'd accepted a payoff in return for his killing them. I felt responsible to see it was used wisely, the way they would have."

Zac nodded. Did he really understand?

The silence stretched between them. Abby

wanted to jump to her feet and race away. The rest of the group were gathered around the fire, softly singing. They couldn't possibly have heard her admissions, but she still felt vulnerable.

"I get it. But I also think you wanted the control." Zac seemed to be looking directly at her, though she knew he couldn't see past his eye coverings. "You wanted one tiny portion of your life where no one could tell you—er, force you to do anything," he continued in a flat, clear voice.

"Yes." She said it almost defiantly.

They sat beside each other in silence for a few minutes. Then Zac's hand reached out to grasp hers. Abby felt his fingers tighten around hers for a fraction of a second. A shiver of relief filled her. She was safe with Zac, no longer the silly idiot who'd married a man who never really loved her at all.

"You needed control because Ken abused you."

The words rocked her world. She felt exposed, unable to hide under the familiar mantle of self-control.

"Ken never hit me, if that's what you're implying." She struggled to regain her composure.

"It isn't. He didn't have to hit you to abuse you." Zac's words were hard, as if they were bitten off and spit out. His fingers now squeezed hers so tightly she dragged her hand free. "There are all kinds of abuse, Abby. The worst kind is often inflicted using language. Some men like that method because it's much harder to defend against. Did Ken call you names, demean you?"

She pulled her sweater around her body more tightly, chilled though the evening was warm and the fire provided extra heat. "I don't want to talk about it."

"I don't blame you. Verbal abuse is hard to rout from our minds. When we're most vulnerable, least prepared to defend ourselves from those who are supposed to love us, it echoes inside our head and tells us we're not who we think we are." Zac shook his head. "But the voice is wrong, Abby. Ken was wrong. You were not selfish or any of the other things he no doubt called you."

"We should have shared the money," she mumbled.

"Why? Because Ken always shared with you?" He paused, then asked, "He didn't want you to go to that market you talked about, did he? Because you'd spend too much?"

"He said the vendors cheated me." She hadn't meant to answer. The words just seemed to pour out of her. "They didn't, though. Bargaining is common, but I never liked to do it. Those people were so poor. How could I begrudge them a few cents more in payment for such backbreaking labor? They became my friends," she whispered.

"Because you couldn't have any friends come

to your home," he guessed, not even waiting for her acknowledgment. "Because Ken wanted you home alone, with Levi, without anyone who could support you, whom you could lean on or confide your troubles in."

"Yes."

"That's why he insisted you live in Botswana, though your parents lived far away?" Zac's lips pursed at her nod. "Ken was wrong to treat you like that, Abby. *He* was wrong. Not you. I'm guessing you shut up and tried your hardest to make things work, didn't you? You kept the peace."

"It was easier," she admitted.

"Easier, perhaps, since you had no defender," Zac murmured. "But it was actually very costly. So costly that you now believe you can't spend any of your money on yourself, to make your own life easier or more pleasant."

In the distance, Abby could hear the twins say something to their grandfather, but it got lost in Zac's next comment.

"Whatever he said and did was from personal interest and it was not true. You are alive, you are healthy and you control your own future," he insisted. "Ken has no place in your life, no call on your emotions, no say about what you do now. You deserve to be happy, Abby. You deserve to enjoy your life, to give yourself the opportunity to live fully, savoring the blessings you've been given. Including that money." He paused as his hand found her arm and rested there, his touch warming her cool skin. "Wouldn't your parents be thrilled to know that you aren't depriving yourself, but really living, thanks to the legacy they left?"

"I—I never thought of it that way."

Their conversation was broken up by the twins, who urged their father to try the s'mores they'd just made. The others followed, sinking into the surrounding chairs and sharing laughter and jokes, happy to be together, including Abby as if she belonged.

It wasn't until they were back in the log house, the twins asleep with happy smiles on their faces, that she again found herself alone with Zac. But she wanted to escape, to think about what he'd said. She said good night and had her hand on the doorknob when his voice stopped her.

"Abby?"

"Yes?"

"Don't let Ken take up any more space in your head. Don't let the memory of his accusations or his greed color your future. Push it away so you can wrap yourself in today and all that it has to offer."

"I'll try." She opened the door, then paused. "Those are words you should live by, too, Zac.

Because surely if God has plans for me, He also has plans for you?"

"I'm counting on it, though it's a little difficult right now to understand what they could be," he shot back, a wry smile tipping his lips.

"'I know the plans I have for you,'" she quoted.

"Yeah." He sank into his easy chair with a sigh.

Abby turned to leave. But a question lingered.

"How did you know?" she asked.

"About Ken abusing you?" He inclined his head. "Peace Meadow. You lavished the place with love, yet you don't lavish yourself. It was the most likely explanation given the few things you'd told me about him."

"Oh." She turned to leave.

"Also, I counseled abused women on that help line I told you about. I'm afraid it's a pervasive issue in this country," he murmured.

"You see more with your eyes bandaged than Ken ever saw with twenty-twenty vision," she told him. "That's what makes you such a great counselor, Zac."

Then she closed the door and went to her room to think about those moments when he'd taken her hand and how her heart had thumped so hard she'd thought it would burst. The words he'd spoken, his encouragement and support—it felt as if he'd lifted away a huge weight and allowed her to escape from under it.

She *would* refocus on living today and leave Ken in the past. And she'd pray that God would show her how to enjoy her life once more. But not only her. Zac needed to find a new purpose in his life, too.

Abby tried not to think about how hard it would be to leave the Double H and the wonderful people who'd entered her world. She'd just have to keep talking to God about it and keep reminding Zac that he wasn't alone, no matter how he felt.

Chapter Eight

May brought lengthening days, and Abby began to feel deep satisfaction in her life at Hanging Hearts Ranch. At Mandy's insistence, she learned to ride in the evenings, after the girls had retired, before she read to Zac. Delighted by her accomplishments, she pressed him to let Drew give the twins preliminary lessons, too. Zac remained adamantly opposed.

"I want to teach them myself," he kept insisting. "When I can see."

Would he ever see again? And when would that be? Twice she'd driven Zac to see an ophthalmologist, and twice she'd heard the doctor's advice. *Wait a few weeks more.*

Abby did not find that advice heartening. Zac's frustration increased, his anger at God's lack of help pouring out on the ride home.

"Why aren't they healing? Does God want me

blind?" he'd demanded. "What am I supposed to do if I'm blind?"

She didn't argue or try to soothe him. She felt he needed to vent without worrying that his family would hear him and grow more concerned. With no way to work off his frustration, no way to go for a ride into the forest like Ben or chop wood as Mandy said Drew did, Abby helped the only way she knew, by encouraging him to join her and the twins for daily walks around the ranch. And she prayed, pleading with God to heal this man she feared she was growing to care for.

It was after one of these prayer sessions, as she was returning from Peace Meadow, that Abby saw Zac and one of the ranch hands, Oliver, sitting on the deck, seemingly in deep conversation. Hesitant to interrupt, she walked toward the main house to see if Bonnie wanted help in her garden.

"Hello, dear. Enjoying your free morning?" Bonnie's cheerful face always made the day seem better. "By the sounds of the girls, the children's choral presentation next Sunday is going to be fantastic."

"The twins have been practicing their songs nonstop." Abby bent and began pulling weeds. "I see Zac's busy," she said, striving for nonchalance.

"He and Oliver have talked several times lately. Zac also met with another, younger hand when you were out with the girls." Bonnie chuckled. "My guess is both cases are about a woman."

"Oh?" So not what she'd imagined.

"The two of them looked lovesick to me." Bonnie chuckled as she flexed her fingers, covered in work gloves. "Zac's at his best when he's dealing in human relationships. He always seems able to encourage people. He's known how since he first came to us. Grace—Miss Partridge—noticed his gift right off. Maybe because he often chose her library to inspire his chums. Say, have you seen her lately?"

"Not since the other afternoon when we worked on your quilt. Why?" Abby asked.

"It's probably nothing." Bonnie paused, her face thoughtful. "I just thought that recently she's seemed—I don't know—down?"

"It's funny you should say that. I've had the same feeling," Abby told her. "I thought I was being fanciful."

"Understandable you would think so since she doesn't often get down. But somehow Grace seems—well, sad isn't quite the right word. Maybe depressed?" Bonnie sighed. "A lot of folks in town shun her because she has a reputation as a gossip. She's been trying hard to change that, but this is a tight-knit community where reputations aren't easily altered. I mean, we've all known each other for ages."

"And Miss P.—that's what Zac calls her—as a nongossip doesn't fit in?" Abby frowned. "Maybe you'll think it's silly, but I told Zac I think she's lonely."

"You know, I believe that may just be it!" Bonnie grinned. "You have the same heart for people as Zac, Abby."

"Oh, no. I'm just guessing." But the other woman shook her head.

"It's not all head knowledge. It also takes heart knowledge, being able to discern when something isn't right with another person." She attacked the dirt more vigorously. "I need to pray about it and listen in case the Lord has something for me to do to help Grace."

"Oliver's leaving so I guess I'd better get back to Zac and finish reading that medical journal he's interested in. Or do you want me to stay and help you even though I haven't much knowledge about gardening?"

"No, dear, you go keep Zac company." Bonnie patted her shoulder. "The garden has always been my best thinking spot. Maybe you could get his thoughts back on Grace. My son might have a good suggestion about how to help her."

"Great idea. I'll do that. And please feel free to ask if you want my help. That's what I'm here for," Abby told her.

"You're already helping all of us so much.

We're so grateful for you, Abby." After a hug, Bonnie returned to her work.

Abby dumped her weeds in a pile by the potting bench, let herself out of the fenced garden and walked across the yard toward Zac.

"You've been busy," she said as she climbed the steps. "Ready for a coffee break?"

"Yes," he said, rising to follow her inside.

"Your mom said she thinks Oliver was talking to you about a lady."

His shout of laughter made her pause in her coffee preparations to turn and stare at him.

"I wish I knew how she does that," he said, sitting down at the breakfast bar.

"So she's right?" She bit her lips when he shook his head. "Never mind. I know it's confidential." She waited a moment for the coffee to drip through, trying to think of a way to broach the subject of Miss P.

"Mom's in her garden?" He laughed when she nodded. "I think she goes there so much so she can keep an eye on all of us. I always figured that's why she loves gardening." Zac inclined his head. "You're awfully quiet. What's wrong?"

"Nothing's wrong." Abby exhaled. "But something is bothering me. Bonnie thought maybe you could help."

"If I can." He accepted his mug of coffee and took a sip. "Perfectly creamed, thank you."

"It's Miss Partridge. Both Bonnie and I think she's seemed down lately." She sat opposite him, liking how easy it was to talk to him.

"Down? You mean depressed?" His forehead pleated as he considered it.

"Maybe. Or lonely." Abby rushed on to stop him from interrupting. "I know Miss P. has been a gossip in the past, but your mother says she's trying to change. Maybe she realizes no one trusts her or believes she has changed. I don't know. She just seems…dispirited?"

"Huh. I wouldn't know." Zac took one of the cookies she offered and bit into it. After a moment he paused, lifted his head and seemed to look directly at her. "You want me to do something. I can hear the gears in your brain turning. But what can I do?"

"Talk to her?" she suggested. "She knows and likes you. Maybe she'll open up and discuss whatever's bothering her and we can somehow help her."

"Abby." Zac huffed out a sigh. "I've only kept talking to Leo because he seems so desperate."

"And you've helped him. He told me that last Sunday," she blurted. "You must be helping Oliver and the other guy, too, or they wouldn't keep coming back to talk to you. You have a gift for listening and offering practical advice. So why not talk to Miss P., as well? What could it hurt?"

Just then a solid rap sounded at the door. It opened to reveal the very person they'd been discussing.

"Am I interrupting something?" Miss Partridge asked, glancing from one to the other.

"We were just having coffee," Abby said, and quickly added, "But I've got some errands—oh." She glanced at her phone and groaned. "Excuse me. I have to leave."

"What's wrong?" Zac demanded. "The twins?"

"It's a text from Mandy. She's not feeling well. I'll have to go take her place at the kids' practice. Remember what we discussed, Zac." She snatched up the keys, waved to Miss Partridge and scurried out, relieved that the two would have an opportunity to talk alone.

Zac would probably chide her later, but she didn't care. Miss Partridge needed to talk to someone. Abby was sure of it. And whether Zac was willing to admit it or not, he was the perfect person to listen.

Funny how he couldn't see that.

"You probably think I'm a silly old woman who has read too many romance novels."

Zac shook his head at Miss Partridge, although in truth he had wondered what had put this latest idea into her head.

"Maybe I have, but for most of my life I've

been so busy. Now suddenly I have time since I'm retired, but I don't have anyone to spend it with." She paused. "No, that's not right. I mean, I don't have anyone special to share my life with. And I'd like to. Is that stupid?"

"Why would it be stupid?" he asked automatically. "Doesn't everyone want somebody to share things with?"

"So? How do I find him?" she demanded.

"Sorry?" Zac was glad his eyes were covered so she couldn't see his shock.

"Him. The one I want to share my future with. How do I find him?" There was a sound of pouring. "I've refilled your cup and poured one for myself. I hope you don't mind." She didn't wait to see if he did but pressed on with her questions. "I've heard about putting an advertisement on the internet. Should I try that?"

He gulped, stunned by her suggestion.

"Well, Zac?" she demanded when he didn't immediately respond. "I've never known you at a loss for words."

"I'm—er, thinking," he managed to say. *You're going to pay for this, Abby.* "Maybe first you should decide what you want in this person who would share your life."

"Oh, I know all that. My age, my faith, retired, willing to travel, self-supporting." She sounded satisfied, as if she'd nailed down all the important things.

Zac couldn't suppress a smile.

"What's so funny?" she demanded.

"Miss Partridge, if a man walked into this house right now with all those, um, qualities, would that automatically make him the man of your dreams?"

"Well, it's a start." She hummed for a moment. "What else should I consider?"

"Well, how about education? You've run a library and done a lot of reading so I think a common interest in books might be important to you." Since he couldn't see if she was nodding, he continued. "I think you'd prefer someone who has a music interest, too, because you've been involved in the church music ministry for as long as I've known you."

"So I should look for those things. Okay." He heard the sound of scratching.

"Are you writing this down?" *Oh, Lord, what am I doing here?*

"Of course. Then I can take out my list and check it against men in church."

"No!" Zac modulated his voice while fighting the fear that she'd tell the community he'd told her how to look for a man. "That isn't what I meant." He scrounged for a better way to explain. "May I tell you how Maria and I met?" he said finally.

"At med school, wasn't it?" Miss Partridge sounded smug.

"Anatomy class, to be exact. Our professor asked me to tutor her." He smiled at the memory. "I thought she was dumb because she couldn't keep the foot bones straight. She thought I was arrogant and overconfident."

"Meaning?" Miss P. had never had time for what she called lollygagging.

"Meaning that it took time and getting to know each other before we realized all we had in common. Neither of us had a list we checked off and then decided to get married," he clarified. "We had to figure out what we admired about the other person and come to terms with the things that bothered us. And there were a lot of things."

"You didn't like Maria?" she asked, sounding confused.

"Of course I liked her. I fell in love with her. But no one is totally loveable. We all have flaws and foibles." He could almost hear her confusion in her silence. "We're wonderfully and intricately made, the Bible says. But people are like pieces of a puzzle. Sometimes the pieces just won't fit together no matter how much you want them to."

"Like you and that girl you dated in high school. Jenny Parker," Miss Partridge murmured as she nodded. "She was most unsuitable for you."

"Why?" he asked, nonplussed that she'd remembered his past dating partners.

"For one thing, you've always been a people person, like Abby is." Miss P. sounded indignant. "The two of you care about others. You both go out of your way to help whenever you can."

Zac shifted uncomfortably under the comparison. "You don't think Jenny did?"

"Jenny was concerned about Jenny," the lady stated in disgust. "She didn't have time to coach her classmates or encourage anyone. She was too self-involved. I never understood why it took you forever to see that."

"I guess." He wasn't sure where this was leading, but it felt like he'd lost control of the discussion.

"And that Emily girl. She was awful for you!"

"Emily?" He didn't even remember anyone named Emily!

"She wouldn't even look at your mother's petting zoo, said she was terrified of animals. More like the smell." Miss P. didn't hide her disgust. "You're a rancher's son. You brought her to the family ranch. Who doesn't expect there to be animals on a ranch?"

"Yes, well." Zac needed to redirect the discussion. "My point is, you can't choose a life partner the same way you use a shopping list to get groceries."

"I don't see why not," she protested. "It's seems a perfectly sensible way to me."

"And how has that worked so far?" he demanded, exasperated that she couldn't or wouldn't understand. "We're talking about emotions here and emotions aren't always rational. I'll give you an example. A perfectly rational choice of a partner for you, in my opinion, would be a retired banker or businessman."

"Why?" she asked immediately.

"Well, several reasons. You've never lived on a ranch and I doubt you'd want to take second place to the demands and necessities a rancher deals with, or that you'd like it if he had to cancel a trip because an issue came up with his cattle. So I said businessman. If he's retired, he's finished with work. He would be free to travel."

"Like Grady La Strange. He worked at the bank for years. But he lives with his mother." Zac could almost see her shaking her head. "Essie is lovely but I don't want to live with her."

"Okay." He nodded. "And you probably don't want to live with your partner's other family members, either. Right?"

"You mean their children?" Miss P. was silent for a moment before earnestly explaining, "I like children. I do. But I think I'm too old to move in with a young child or a teenager."

"See? Now you're starting to narrow your field,

to figure out what you really want in a mate." He felt a flutter of satisfaction at his success so far.

"What about food?" she demanded.

Completely confused, Zac simply said, "Food?"

"Yes. I don't care to experiment with dried worms or fried spiders or anything like that." He heard no wavering in that no-nonsense tone he knew so well.

"But you said you want to travel," he objected. "What about foreign cuisine?"

"I have no objection to French or Italian," she told him in a very prim voice.

"Meaning you want to travel with someone who won't expect you to visit very exotic places. Okay, now, what about the way you travel? Hiking the Swiss Alps? Backpacking the Outback? Bus tours? Cruises?"

"Ooh, I've always wanted to cruise the Rhine," she said dreamily. "I'm beginning to understand what you mean, Zac. I need to be more focused about what I expect from a partner, and what I will and won't tolerate."

"Tolerate wasn't exactly—" He gave up trying to explain his intended meaning at the sound of her footsteps tapping across the hardwood floor. "Miss Partridge?" he called.

"Just pulling on my sweater," she said. "Thank

you so much for your help, dear. You've given me very clear direction of the path I want to pursue."

"Um—" Zac hesitated, but in the end he knew he had to just say it. Otherwise he'd have steered the woman totally wrong. "*Pursuing* may not be exactly the way to go about things," he warned.

"No, of course not." He heard the door creak open and waited, hoping she wouldn't just leave. Relief surged when she spoke again. "Our talk has narrowed my perspective, made me reconsider the men I've chosen as possible candidates."

Still not what he'd aimed for. Zac opened his mouth to restate but Miss P. spoke first.

"I'm not sure how Abby does it," she said thoughtfully.

"Abby?" He frowned, trying not to stiffen. Surely she wasn't going to criticize his nurse. "What do you mean? Does what?"

"Gets everyone to notice her. She's stunning, so naturally everyone stops and stares at her, especially men. They seem to flock to her," Miss P. said wistfully. Then she hurriedly added, "But it's not just Abby's physical beauty. She has this— what should I call it? Poise? Inner direction? Maybe confidence?"

"Sometimes people seem outwardly confident but hide their inner doubts," Zac said quietly.

"Not Abby. I don't know how to phrase it, but she's so warm and friendly. Whenever I speak with her, I have this certainty that she will listen, understand and offer a helpful response to whatever I tell her." The lady sighed. "I wish I was more like her. Abby is someone very special and we are blessed that she's come to live among us."

Having said her piece, Miss Partridge departed, leaving the door open so the sun warmed his face.

A longing to *see* Abby for himself swept over Zac. He felt he knew her well. After all, they spent a lot of time together, both because of the twins and while she treated his eyes. But she also read to him and shared her thoughts on the medical journals. She kept him up to date on what was happening around the ranch, told him if the girls needed something and arranged projects so he could engage with his children and share their world in a small way despite his blindness.

And yet, Miss Partridge's comments made him feel that aside from realizing she'd been abused, he'd never probed beneath the surface, had only occasionally seen past the person Abby showed to the world, the put-together woman his guest had just described.

Somewhere deep inside, the urge grew into a desperate need to understand exactly who Abby was, almost in the same way Miss Partridge wanted to find a soul mate, someone who understood her with all the pretense stripped away.

So Zac had to ask himself if that meant he was

ready to get involved in a personal relationship with Abby, more personal than anything they'd shared thus far?

Wait! Something inside him screamed a reminder that he shouldn't push forward until he found out if he'd ever see again.

Of course, if Abby was as beautiful as everyone said, she'd hardly want to be involved with a blind man.

Chapter Nine

The following week, Abby sat on the deck of the log house enjoying a midmorning break with Zac, amazed by how natural it felt to be here, with him.

"Your parents are healing so well," she said, spying the couple working together in the garden. "When I applied ointment on your mom's arms yesterday, I noticed she's regained almost complete dexterity in her fingers and wrists."

"And Dad?" Zac leaned forward, obviously concerned.

"Oh, he's also doing great. He even insisted on wearing his cowboy boots yesterday." She chuckled. "I think that once Ben got those battered boots back on his feet, he felt less like an invalid, as he so disparagingly called it, and more like the ranch boss man."

"Yeah. They were both lucky." Zac frowned, cupping his mug in his hands as he spoke.

"No, they *are* blessed," she corrected firmly. "God has been with them the whole time, Zac."

"Except when it happened," he muttered, but not so quietly that she didn't hear.

"You know that isn't true." Abby couldn't let his negativity pass. "You say that, but you of all people know the truth of God's presence. He is with us all the time. You've experienced it in your own life, I'm sure. Yet you keep clinging to this—this grudge against God." She couldn't stop herself from reminding him, "Stuff happens, Zac, but the speed bumps in life don't define our faith or God. It's what we do with the bad stuff that matters."

Zoe and Mia played happily on the nearby swing set, squealing with joy as they soared upward. Their laughter was music to Abby's ears. His children seemed to have let go of any bad memories. Why couldn't Zac?

"It's not that easy for me to simply accept that I had to lose my eyesight or that my parents had to suffer horribly when they were burned in the tack barn fire. God *let* it happen. He for sure didn't stop it." A muscle in his jaw flickered. "You're going to remind me that I saw suffering a thousand times before in my work and managed to deal with it when it was someone else. So why can't I accept it in my own life?" He grimaced. "I don't know why, but I just can't accept that God allowed those guerillas to destroy everything."

"I didn't say it would be easy to move past," she assured him soothingly. "Only—are you sure it isn't more a case of *I won't forget*? I overheard you suggest to Leo that he concentrate on the future. You don't think the same advice applies to you?"

"Maybe." Zac shrugged it off, clearly unwilling to discuss it further.

"Can I ask you something?" Abby wasn't finished. She waited for his nod before asking, "What happens if in, say, six months, you still don't have an answer to why God allowed your mission to be destroyed or you to be injured? What if you don't have your sight back by then?"

"I don't have an answer," he whispered, sounding forlorn.

Abby's heart ached for him, but she wouldn't give up on him. Sightless or not, Zac had so much to give, if he could only see it. What she now felt compelled to say would be hard for Zac to hear, but she had to help him move beyond this crossroad where he was stuck.

"Let's look at this a different way. Say that tomorrow your eye specialist takes off the bandages and you can see as well as you could before. What will you do? You can't go back into missions work, or probably any kind of ministry, with your trust in God unresolved." Though he winced, she continued. "Or is regaining your sight reason enough for you to forgive God for breaking your trust, for allowing pain and hurt into your life? If you and your family get back to normal, will that be enough to make you trust God again? And if not, what will?"

"You sure have a way with words, Abby," he said tersely. "The answer is, I don't know." His jaw worked soundlessly until he finally demanded, "How am I supposed to trust God after all this?"

"How can you not trust Him when He kept you and your daughters safe through terrible turmoil?" she demanded. "You speak as if there's an alternative to trust, but for a Christian there isn't. If you don't trust God, with everything," she emphasized, "then who or what do you trust? Yourself? We both know the folly of that."

"It's just that I thought—" He stopped.

"What?" Abby finally gave voice to something that had stewed in her mind for days. "You thought that Zac the missionary would be above the hurt? That Maria's death was enough of a sacrifice? That God wouldn't let anything else happen to you?"

"Yes," he blurted, his face strained. "I thought that leaving home, going without all the conveniences other Christians enjoy, watching my wife die while we were doing *God's* work…" He gulped, exhaled and spoke again, but in a more controlled tone. "I stupidly thought those sacrifices would be enough for God. Guess I was wrong." The side of his mouth tipped in a sardonic smile. "Stupid me."

"Zac—"

"Please don't repeat the *all things work together for good* verse, Abby," he begged. "No matter how I try, I simply cannot find the good in this." He pointed to his covered eyes.

"I wasn't going to say you should," she chided softly. "I was going to say that God loves you. Whether you believe it or not, whether you feel it or not, it is true. What you've gone through, what you're going through now, doesn't change that."

Her soul wept for all he'd lost, but especially for the loss of his trust in God's love. Zac was hurting and who could blame him? If only she could draw him into her arms and somehow comfort him. But that was impossible. Though she'd grown to care deeply for this man, pain and fear from her past wouldn't allow her to give her heart again. All she had to offer were words, promises she'd clung to when her own world had crashed around her.

"You are God's precious child, Zac," she said, threading her fingers in his. "He chose you because He loves you. He knows every detail of the work you've done. He has noted every sacrifice you've made. He's not punishing you. He's working through His plan. His, not yours or mine or someone else's. Please hang on until He's completed His plan."

He said nothing, though his fingers tightened around hers. The birds sang, the wind whispered across the grass, tossing it to and fro, while crickets chirped their repetitive song. Abby heard it all as background while she silently prayed for him.

Then a loud squeal splintered their solitude.

"What's wrong?" Zac demanded, releasing her hand as he jerked upright.

"Mia fell off the swing," Abby explained as she rose. "She's fine. More shocked than anything, I think. I'll be back in a minute."

After she'd soothed Mia's bump, she served the girls a picnic snack of lemonade and cookies on the grass with their father. Then Ella arrived and Zac returned to the deck. Abby wondered if she should continue their discussion, but before she could, he'd plunged into a new topic.

"Fixing up Peace Meadow was a great idea of yours, Abby, especially since Miss Partridge keeps sending me more people to talk to." He sipped his coffee thoughtfully. "It's great to have a space away from those two rambunctious ones. They make it impossible to talk to anyone here, let alone expect them to reveal their innermost thoughts. Now I can run away to the meadow. Or at least walk," he corrected cynically.

"Do I hear a but in there somewhere?" She loved his grin, those times when a hint of cheeky humor tilted his lips, erasing all trace of melancholy from his face.

"Not a but, *but…*" He chuckled as he leaned back. "The thing is, I have to keep bothering people to get me there and then ask whomever I'm talking to if they'll bring me back here." He sighed. "You wouldn't know this, but the meadow was always my go-to hideaway when I was a kid. I'd bury myself in the trees. I often dreamed of Peace Meadow when I was in Africa. The calm and serenity—well, some days I have a yen to stay there by myself, just sit and reflect on things until I feel like coming back."

"Funny, I was thinking about that yesterday when I was late coming to get you." Abby smothered her excitement at the plan she'd already conceived. "I actually had an idea when we first saw the chairs at the hardware store, but I forgot about it. I'll show you what I have in mind after supper, okay?"

"Now I'm curious," Zac said, both eyebrows raised.

"Good." Abby changed the subject. "How are you feeling about seeing the doctor tomorrow?"

"Like it's a huge nuisance. I hate having to drag you there and ruin your entire day for what will probably be another wait-and-see prescription." He shuffled his feet so his legs stretched out in front of him. "I suppose it's rather like you trying to plan your future when you haven't any clue how long you'll be stuck here. We're both spinning our wheels while the world rolls on around us."

"Hey! I am *not* stuck here," she corrected him. "I choose to be here, and I can't think of a lovelier place or more wonderful people to be *stuck* with. The Double H is fascinating. Yesterday I saw a baby horse's arrival into the world."

"Foal," he corrected, and then frowned. "It's a bit late in the season for that."

"Yes, so Mandy said. I think the mother—"

"Dam," he corrected again. "And the father horse is called a sire."

"I think the *dam* was older. She had a hard time." There was so much to learn at Hanging Hearts Ranch. Abby wondered if she'd ever get it right. "Anyway, the birth was a sight to behold." Zac made a face. "What? Didn't I say it right?"

"Foaling. The foaling was a sight to behold." He grinned. "Aren't all births amazing? Like a promise for the future. At least, that's how I felt when the twins arrived, and with every child I ever delivered."

"I felt the same with Levi," she murmured, reminded of the rush of joy that had swelled each time she cuddled her son or gazed on his tiny face. "Precious gifts," she whispered, swallowing hard to stop the tears.

Zac said nothing, his head tilted to one side as if he was studying her. They both started at the sound of a motor shattering the silence.

"Is it Miss P.? Again?" he asked dryly. "She'll pretend she came to see me, but she'll somehow slip in a comment about Avery Kent, who's feeling down since his dad died, or Arianna Parker, who's thinking about running away from home because her parents are separating, or Nelda Cross whose kid is leaving for college in the fall and she can't bear to contemplate her empty nest."

"Wow! How do you know all this stuff?" Abby asked, stunned.

"It's only my sight that doesn't work, you know. I hear very well. Especially at church. But even if I didn't, Miss P. keeps showing up here, pretending she's come to see how I am, but it's actually to talk about her list of 'husband prospects' with whom she wants me to meet." He grimaced. "If I tell you something," he murmured as the vehicle's motor shut off. "Will you promise not to gloat?"

"Maybe." Abby caught the faint flicker of a grin at the corner of his mouth. "You're actually enjoying talking about her *prospects*, aren't you?"

"Zac, dear! How are you?" Miss Partridge called, interrupting their discussion.

"Keep that to yourself, Abby," he ordered, but he was smiling as he replied in a louder voice, "I'm good, Miss Partridge. And you?"

"Fine as frog's hair. Hello, Abby. I came to talk to Zac about someone who wants to ask him about mission work." Miss Partridge paused when Ella, Mia and Zoe rushed over. "My dears, hello," she greeted them with a huge smile. "May they have a treat, Zac?"

"Chocolate bars," Abby explained sotto voce as Miss Partridge drew three from the capacious quilted bag she always carried.

"I'm sure they'd love it, wouldn't you, girls?" Zac's reminder to use their manners was implicit in his tone.

"Yes! Thank you," the children said in unison. They found a shady spot under the newly leafed cottonwood tree to enjoy their snack.

"Who is this intrepid new missionary?" Zac's voice now had an edge that hadn't been there before.

"She's a junior who has been actively involved in several summer youth missions. She speaks two languages fluently and is working on a third. Her name is Melanie." Miss Partridge huffed out the words as if she was out of breath from climbing stairs.

"Have a seat, Miss Partridge," Abby said. "Would you like some coffee?"

"Perhaps a glass of something cool," the lady said. "I've been rushing so much today."

Abby went to fetch it. When she returned, Zac and his guest were glaring at each other. At least, that's what it looked like, except Zac's eyes were covered. Still, the rest of his demeanor showed anger or perhaps frustration. No, make that belligerence.

"I don't want to talk to anyone about Africa," he snapped, his body rigid. "This Melanie person should contact the mission society."

"Melanie has already done that and they've told her what they can. What she's after now is a firsthand view of day-to-day life in another country. She has a ton of questions, Zachary," Miss Partridge said in a wheedling voice. "You must know how difficult it is to anticipate some things. Wouldn't you have appreciated someone telling you to bring your favorite candy bar from home or informing you that your favorite tea wouldn't be available?"

"I do not want to talk about Africa," he repeated through gritted teeth. "Not now. Maybe not ever."

"Hmm." Miss Partridge flopped back in her chair and took a deep drink of her iced tea. She waited, as if she thought he'd change his mind, and when he didn't, she sighed heavily. "All right, then. Never mind." She thanked Abby for the beverage and rose. "I must get on with my day. Oh, dear. I almost forgot."

"Forgot what?" Zac asked in a grumpy tone.

"CDs," Miss Partridge said triumphantly. "A friend found a source of those medical journals you like. They're voice recordings of old and new material. I asked for the last two years and they arrived today. I'll get them for you."

"The last two years?" Zac looked stunned. "I had no idea they'd recorded—"

"Neither did I. Praise the Lord for friends willing to help." She started down the stairs. Abby quickly joined her.

"I'll help you. Girls," she called to the twins. "Would you like to give us a hand?" She winked at Miss P. "It makes them feel they're part of things if they pitch in now and again."

"Well, of course it does." The former librarian handed each of the girls a small package and told them to take it to Zac. When they left, she didn't immediately hand another package to Abby. "Have I done something to anger him?" she asked worriedly.

"No. It's just that Zac hasn't quite dealt with all that happened in Africa," she said, not wanting to break his confidence. "Give him a while and

I'm sure he'll be willing to talk to your student. But we mustn't press him. Healing takes time."

It wasn't the first time she'd said that, Abby reflected as she watched Miss Partridge drive away. And it wouldn't be the last. Healing from a physical wound happened much faster than the healing of damaged hearts and souls.

"Abby?" Zac called.

She carried the last packet of CDs to him.

"That was very kind of Miss P.," she said. "Now you won't be forced to listen to me mangle those medical terms I've never heard of."

"You never mangle anything." He inclined his head. It felt as if he was studying her, except of course, he couldn't see. "Did I offend her?"

So each was worried about the other. Abby felt somewhat better about the woman's visit.

"I don't think she's offended. She's excited about helping Melanie, but I'm sure she understands your hesitations."

"I hope so." He stretched out once more.

She was too aware of this man, of the piney scent of his aftershave, of the flop of hair over his forehead and of the nuances of his moods. She cared deeply that he still suffered over the events of the past and feared reminders might force him to relive them again mentally. To stop herself from offering unwanted comfort, she stepped toward the door.

"I think the girls and I should get busy making lunch. Do you want me to set up one of those CDs for you to listen?"

"No, thanks," he said absently. "I'll just sit here and listen to the birds for a while."

And maybe pray?

Don't hope for the impossible, Abby.

Zac could barely contain his curiosity about Abby's promised after-supper surprise, more so since she'd disappeared this afternoon for well over an hour and not even the twins knew where she'd gone. Relieved when the meal was over, dishes done and no other excuse to delay them, he gladly followed her outside.

"I like s'prises," Zoe announced.

"Me, too," Mia chanted. "Don't you, Daddy?"

It sounded as if the pair were dancing circles around him, which was somewhat disorienting when he couldn't see them.

"Okay, girls. I want you to promise there will be no talking for the next five minutes. Okay?" Abby waited, apparently received the confirmation she wanted and then took his hand. "Ready, Zac?"

Funny how the mere touch of her fingers on his skin settled the rush of nerves that gripped him. Or was it the calming sound of her voice? Either way, he relaxed and nodded.

"Good. You've taken the last step and are now on solid ground. I want you to find the last railing post." She moved his hand forward and then let go.

"Oh, Daddy—"

"Girls! No speaking, remember?" Abby's stern voice hushed the twins.

More curious than ever now, Zac reached out, felt the top of the newel post at the foot of the stairs. He slid his hand over it, wondering what this was about. A moment later his fingers felt a thick cord tied around the wood.

"What's this?" he asked. "Rope? Why?"

"Let's just follow it," Abby suggested. "You lead."

"Really?" He gave her his most carefree smile while his heart thudded double time. "Me? Lead? You do realize I can't see?"

"Uh-huh. Use the rope to guide you."

"Okay." Shrugging, he slid his hand along the rope and slowly walked forward. Then he felt a bump or a knot and stopped. "Is this the end?"

"No." Abby laughed. "It's a marker to warn you that the level of the path is about to change. How does it feel?"

"Like there's a massive knot in it," he said, his fingers moving over it curiously.

"The larger the knot, the bigger the change in the slope will be. Let's keep going," she encouraged.

The longer Zac walked with his hand on the

rope, the more comfortable he became. He stumbled now and again, but the rope supported him. The path seemed fairly even and he guessed Abby had enlisted Drew's help to grade and newly gravel it.

"We're going to Peace Meadow," he guessed.

"Can we talk now?" Zoe demanded, sounding utterly disgruntled.

"Yeah, can we?" Mia echoed.

"Sure." Abby laughed, a musical sound that added to Zac's confident strides. "Just remember to walk on this side of your dad so he can keep hold of the rope."

"This is a funny s'prise, isn't it, Daddy?" Disappointment echoed in Zoe's words.

"It's a great surprise, sweetheart," Zac told her.

"Why?" Mia wondered. "It's just a rope."

"Because the rope is here, because Abby made it so I can use it to get around—that's what makes it great," he explained, thrilled that he was able to move ahead so easily.

"Huh." Mia thought about it for a moment, then bellowed, "I'm goin' to the gazebo!" Her sister echoed the comment and their squeals of excitement dimmed as they raced away.

"They're not grateful, but I sure am. It was very kind of you to do this for me, Abby." Zac wasn't sure where she was standing so he addressed the air in front of him. "It's fantastic.

Now I can come here whenever I want, sit for as long as I want and go home when I want. It's a bit of freedom and it feels wonderful."

"Just don't sit in the sun too long," she warned with a laugh.

"I love it out here." Zac felt along the rope and found it fastened to one of the chairs Abby had purchased for the meadow.

"On the other side of your chair, the rope continues to the gazebo," she explained. "Or if you want to sit at the table, there's a second rope that leads to it."

"Perfect." He seated himself, leaned back and sighed. "Absolutely perfect." Then he remembered the twins. "I don't hear the girls. There's a creek behind those trees. If they fall in they'll—"

"The girls are fine. They're sitting in the gazebo, probably telling stories to each other." As usual, a smile was audible in her words. "If you feel to your left, there's a cooler tucked under the table. It has a lock, which will make it very difficult for critters to get into. But it's the perfect place to store drinks and some snacks for you and your guests."

"Especially Leo." Zac grinned cheekily. "That man loves your cookies."

"How's he doing?" Abby asked.

"I've suggested he see a therapist." Zac said it

flatly, wondering if she would think he'd failed. Again.

"Why?" she asked. He heard only interest in her question.

"We've talked extensively and I've suggested a number of things that Leo has done. He's made progress, but in doing so, we've uncovered other issues which I feel require a different type of professional." He folded his arms across his chest. "You want to know something funny?"

"Sure." That was Abby. Always encouraging.

"I was so rusty at counseling that at first all I could think of was to ask him questions, get him talking." He huffed a laugh. "And then, bits of scripture kept floating into my head. I'd repeat them because I didn't have much else to offer him. But according to Leo, those verses had a huge impact on how he has begun to view losing his child. He said they were exactly what he needed, yet I didn't even realize I'd remembered them until the words came out of my mouth. Weird, huh?"

"Not weird at all, Zac." He could hear the laughter in her words. "That's exactly what the Bible promises if we tuck God's words into our hearts. God is using you, even though you don't realize it." Her fingertips brushed across his arm. "I'm very proud of you for helping Leo even though you must have felt overwhelmed. But God wasn't."

The twins raced over and snuggled on his lap, their fingers caressing his cheeks.

"We love you, Daddy," Zoe murmured, her head pressed to his shoulder. "You're our bestest daddy ever."

Mia copied her sister. "The bestest," she agreed.

"I'm also the only daddy you have," Zac murmured with a chuckle, though he clutched his precious daughters nearer.

Contemplating tomorrow terrified him. What if he never saw their faces…? No! He wouldn't think like that.

Abby had reminded him that God had helped with Leo. She'd say God would be there when the bandages came off tomorrow.

Why couldn't he trust God? What did he need to do to rediscover his security in God?

The answers eluded him as they walked home, as they put the twins to bed and as Abby said good night.

"'Casting all your care upon Him; for He careth for you,'" she quoted before she left.

Zac inhaled her fragrance while listening to her footsteps dissipate. Then there was only silence and a breath of air caressing his face.

How was Abby so confident of God's goodness? And why wasn't he?

Chapter Ten

"Can you believe this weekend is Memorial Day?" Abby couldn't stop the words even though they interrupted the CD playing on the car stereo. "Families will be heading off for their first camping weekend. Kids are finishing school. It's so exciting."

"The things that bring you joy constantly amaze me," Zac mumbled. He pushed the button that ejected the CD. It had seemed to grate on his nerves as he'd constantly fidgeted during their drive. She could almost hear his heart begging, *Please let me see today.*

"Bonnie said everyone seems happier with winter gone and the warming sunshine," she said with a shrug. "I think she's right."

"Ah, so winter's departure is what's making you so happy today?" he said, sounding amused by her cheerful tone.

"I've never experienced winter here," Abby reminded him. "Truthfully, I'm a little afraid of it given all your family's horror stories about massive snow dumps and frigid spells that last ages. But I loved the few flurries I saw when we first arrived in New York. And seeing the crocus and daffodils pop up was spectacular, too. So I can say I liked spring very much." She winked at him, knowing he couldn't see it. It felt good to tease him.

"I think you like every time of year. I think you're one of those people who savors the day no matter what the weather is or where you are," Zac mused. "I think carefree Abigail Armstrong just plain enjoys life."

"I used to be carefree." She thought back to the dark days after Levi was gone. She couldn't wish him back, but some days she longed to see his little face again, touch his cheek. Hear his giggle. "That seems like a long time ago. It does feels good to really laugh, though, like when you lost that game you and the girls play." She glanced sideways at him and decided to ask the question that had remained unsaid. "Don't you enjoy life?"

"I'll let you know after today," he muttered.

"It's going to be okay, Zac." She couldn't help reaching over to squeeze his shoulder. "God didn't bring you this far to abandon you. I suppose it's useless to say stop worrying?"

"I wish I could. My confidence level is at an all-time low." He shifted restlessly and rubbed his chest. "I wish I hadn't eaten breakfast."

"There wasn't anything wrong with breakfast. You're nervous, that's all. Lord Jesus, I ask You to comfort Zac right now. Soothe his anxieties. Let him feel Your presence and Your love flowing through him. Help him trust You. Amen." She kept her gaze on the road ahead, hoping her rushed prayer hadn't offended him.

Zac turned to face her. If he could see, Abby knew he'd be staring.

"Do you always do that?"

"Do what? Pray?" She nodded. "Always."

"I mean, out loud? At the drop of a hat," he added.

"You mean do I often blurt out a prayer in the middle of a conversation?" She chuckled as she took the exit toward his doctor's office. "Not usually."

"So why now?" he demanded.

"Because you need God's help. And because I thought—hoped—it might remind you that God is always with us, and that no matter what happens, He'll still be there, loving and supporting us. And to remind you that if we ask Him to build our faith, He'll answer." She eased the car into a parking spot and switched off the motor. "We're here."

"Thank you," Zac said very softly. He made no effort to get out. "I need to be reminded of His love. Being blind—it makes you very self-focused, like you're locked inside this ball where you're the center of the universe and everything is about you." He huffed out a deep breath, then reached out to feel for the door handle. "You continually help me realize life isn't all about me and my issues. You're a special woman, Abby."

A rush of heat flooded Abby's insides as she got out of the car and went to him. She held out her arm so he could place his hand on it, but she didn't move right away. Instead she wasted a few seconds studying the missionary she'd come to admire so much.

"What?" he asked, tipping his head as if he was looking at her.

"*You* are a special man, Zac. You have a gift for relating to people. You listen to everyone, but it occurs to me that I haven't listened enough to you." She debated whether to say it but knew that it was cowardly not to. "You have made a tremendous impact on how I see the world. I value our—" she stopped, hesitated, then said "—friendship very much. You have a lot to give. I hope you'll realize that soon."

Slightly embarrassed that she sounded like a gushing girl, she led him into the building, to the doctor's office. As she did, she silently prayed for guidance and for help. What happened next was going to impact Zac in ways she couldn't even begin to imagine.

Help me to help him, Abby prayed as they sat waiting. Zac's hand touched hers as if he was seeking reassurance. Without even thinking, she threaded her fingers with his.

God, please?

Zac wanted to relax. He wanted to pretend he was confident about the outcome when the doctor uncovered his eyes. He wanted to act like a strong man of faith would act.

Only he wasn't that man.

"Please follow me," the office nurse said.

"Abby?" Zac reached out a hand.

"I'm right here," she murmured as her arm slid under his hand. "The room is about ten paces ahead. Then we turn left."

What would he do without her calming presence, her readiness to do whatever he needed? He didn't want to even think about how uncomfortable his life would be without Abby in it.

Once inside the room, the nurse directed Zac to sit in the big examining chair, same one as last time, he felt certain. When Abby moved away, he experienced a strong sense of loss, as if his anchor was suddenly gone and he was adrift. If he *could* see today, she might start making plans to move on. He hated the thought, the feeling that he'd be alone. Again.

"Good morning," Dr. Faber greeted them a moment later. There was the sound of the door closing before he said, "So today is the day, isn't it, Zac?"

"I guess." Inside he was screaming, *Just get it over with*.

"Let's see how you're doing. Perhaps you'd assist me as before, Nurse Armstrong?" Dr. Faber touched Zac's face with a gloved hand.

"Certainly." Abby's wonderful fragrance suddenly filled Zac's nostrils, and with it a sense of calm flickered inside. She'd be praying for him now.

"First I would like you to switch off the main lights. Over there." A switch snapped. "Good," the doctor said. "Let's begin."

Something, perhaps a towel, was draped across his chest.

"Now, Zac. I'm going to remove these coverings, but I don't want you to open your eyes until I specifically tell you to. First I need to administer some ointment. Your nurse is going to hold your head because the ointment might sting a bit. That's perfectly normal. Ready?" The specialist waited until Zac nodded. "Keep your eyes closed."

Zac obeyed as the doctor freed his eyes from

their bonds. Warm hands—Abby's?—cupped his head on each side. Then his eyelids were lifted individually and something dropped into each eye. Immediately his eyes began to burn.

"Try not to blink for a few minutes," the doctor murmured. "Eyes closed."

It seemed like forever until the stinging finally diminished and Zac could breathe normally again.

"Hmm. Now drops," Dr. Faber decreed.

The drops dribbled into his eyes and ran down his cheeks until Zac longed for the burning to stop. Just as he wished he had something to wipe his streaming face, Abby's hands lifted and he felt the soft press of tissues against his cheeks.

"Don't try to hold back. Let the tears come," Dr. Faber ordered. "Is the burning diminishing now?" Zac nodded and the man continued. "The ointment released the detritus that has accumulated. The drops help soften that and carry it away. Now we must wash and refresh your pupils. Hold still."

Zac wasn't aware he'd moved until Abby's hands tightened once more around his head. These drops soothed and comforted as much as her touch. Both felt so good he sighed with relief.

"The worst is over now. You may release him, Nurse Armstrong." Dr. Faber added, "Thank you for your assistance."

Abby murmured something but Zac was caught up in the light the doctor was shining directly into his eyes. Dr. Faber's low grunting sounds were impossible to decipher.

"I'm going to switch off my examining light now and have Nurse Armstrong open the shade just a bit. When I tell you, I want you to open your eyes. Don't strain, don't pressure yourself. Just glance around. And keep blinking." The doctor paused. "Now."

Zac opened his eyes. At first he could only see smears, probably leftover from the ointment. As directed, he kept blinking, glancing from side to side, and slowly—so slowly—his vision began to clear. Slightly.

Frowning, Zac tried harder to focus. "I can't see much," he said as fear knotted inside him. "Blurs mostly. Some light."

"Normal. All normal," the doctor reassured him. "Don't strain. I want to wash them again."

Once that was over and Abby had dried his face, Zac tried again. This time the shapes in the room were clearer, though cloudiness at the edges remained.

"Is this the best I can hope for?" he demanded, finally giving in to his frustration. "All this waiting, all the treatments, and I still can't see clearly?"

"You must be patient," the doctor began.

"I've been patient," Zac barked. His hands fisted as disappointment swelled. "I—I—"

"Zac." Abby's gentle, reassuring voice cut through the maelstrom inside. "All is well. Be at peace. We haven't finished the race yet, remember? Let Dr. Faber continue."

Somehow her quiet words calmed him. Even more than that, the tender touch of her hand on his pushed away his mushrooming fear that he'd never see as he wanted to, as he had before the attack.

"Sorry," he muttered.

"It's understandable. You thought that once the bandages were off, your sight would be totally restored." The doctor's next words sounded forced. "However, you suffered a great deal of damage to your eyes. I don't believe you will ever fully recover your sight, Zac. Not as it was."

The doctor's words hit like a block of wood to his solar plexus. Zac couldn't think, couldn't imagine, couldn't understand… *Why, God? I wanted so badly to trust You again.*

"Please continue, Doctor." Abby's hand squeezed his. Her serene voice broke through the storm whirling in his mind.

Slowly, exerting great control, Zac exhaled, steeling himself to hear the rest.

"I do believe, however, that your sight will get better than it currently is. It won't be a fast process and you can't hurry it along. You may eventually need another operation." Dr. Farber's face swam into view, a blob of misshapen features Zac slowly blinked into focus. "For the time being, you must wear these dark glasses, both inside and out, while your pupils adjust to light and dark."

Zac blinked as his world suddenly went dark when the doctor slid glasses on his face. But this blindness was a temporary thing. Gradually his eyes began to adjust and he could once more make out shapes, light and dark, which grew more distinct when the doctor fully opened the shade.

"You will have a new prescription for eyedrops. Nurse Armstrong will administer them twice a day. They will help your eyes heal. Other than that, continue as you have been. Keep active, eat well, but most importantly, remain positive. Would you like me to refer you to a counselor or psychologist to help with that?"

"The counselor needs counseling?" The irony was so great that Zac couldn't help but burst into laughter. He saw the doctor turn to look at Abby.

Abby. His vision was *not* perfect. He could not clearly see her, but as she stood in the light from the window, Zac caught his breath. Even with his muddled vision, she was stunning.

"Abby?" he whispered, just to be sure he was focused on the right person.

"Hello, Zac." Her lips creased in a smile that stretched across her face, all the way to her eyes—gloriously wide eyes whose unusual hue he couldn't quite discern, not that it mattered. Her face looked like that of a model. "Pleased to meet you."

Dr. Faber cleared his throat and began speaking, but Zac heard very little of what he said. He was too busy staring, trying to see Abby more clearly, this woman who'd eased everything in his world since the day they'd met. She had made his life bearable.

"That's fine, Doctor. We can do that."

Zac heard Abby say the words, but it was as if he was in a fog. He couldn't stop staring, trying to fully see the woman who had become the ground in his confusing world.

"Come on, Zac. We're finished here for today." Abby's fingers around his wrist brought him out of his stupor. She thanked the doctor, then in her customary no-nonsense fashion slid her arm under his and led him out of the office.

Zac walked beside her, allowing his brain to absorb the shapes and colors, the changing shadows as they moved. Until they reached the exterior door. The sun shone so brightly he had to cover his eyes and allow her to lead him blindly to the car.

"You wanted to see," she reminded him with a grin when they were inside the car.

"Actually, I don't see that well," he complained, grabbing a cap of his father's that lay on the seat between them and slapping it on so the brim shaded his face. "Yet," he added in an attempt to be positive.

"Better?" she asked.

"Much. I find it very bright, though not exactly clear." He tried to surreptitiously study her and found she was looking at him. "Something wrong?"

"You tell me. I know you hoped your sight would be fully restored." She sounded worried.

"Nowhere near that. Let's say I'm better than I was, but I'm not where I want to be."

"Not yet." She nibbled on her bottom lip as she started the car and put it into gear. "He said things will slowly improve."

"He said they *should* slowly improve," Zac corrected, feeling a tightness in his throat. If he couldn't clearly distinguish Abby's features, how could he see Mia and Zoe? How could he be a doctor again?

"Do you mind if we stop for lunch?" Abby asked. "I remember last time we were here I saw a diner a couple of blocks ahead. I'm starving and it's nearly lunchtime. We could eat and then get back on the road."

"Sounds good." Zac wasn't sure he could eat much, but he desperately wanted a cup of coffee. Maybe that would steady this nervous grip that held him captive in his half-sighted world. Would it always be like this?

Abby drove a few blocks, parked and opened her door.

"It's on my side, right?" Zac asked as he clambered out. He kept the brim down and focused on his feet, on stepping onto the sidewalk.

Somehow it hadn't mattered that she'd guided him when he wore the eye coverings. But now they were gone, he was less inclined to lean on her. Which was no doubt silly and vain, but that's how he felt. Exposed, vulnerable and somehow weakened. And determined to prove he was none of those.

"Would it be easier if you had a cane?" Abby asked as she strolled beside him.

"I doubt it." Zac lifted his head enough to see what looked like an upcoming curb. But his depth perception was off, and he couldn't judge how far ahead it was.

"I'm here." As if she understood, Abby slid her arm under his hand and lifted it to her side. "The café is on the next block. Another three steps and then down about six inches. The light is green so we can cross now."

How did she know just when to step in and

when to leave him alone? Zac wondered. Did he have some tell, a certain way of hesitating? Did he look needy to her? He didn't think his steps had faltered but maybe—

"Did you once work with blind people?" he asked on a sudden hunch.

"How did you know?" Abby told him of the upcoming curb and slowed just slightly as he stepped onto the sidewalk again. "I actually did exactly that in my last three years at school. I had this English teacher whom I loved very much. She lost her sight in an accident. She allowed me to attend sessions where she learned to maneuver without sight and agreed to teach me some ways of helping someone who is sightless. She died years ago but I still miss her."

"I'm sorry," Zac murmured.

"Don't be. She's with God, at peace. I'll always be grateful for the lessons she taught me—to enjoy life all the time, wherever you are, whatever is happening. Her name was Violet Sundee and her favorite saying was, 'You'll never get a second chance to relive this day so make the most of it.'"

"And that's what you do, isn't it, Abby?" Zac knew it was true even as he asked. "You see the sunshine in everything. All the time."

"Well, not *all* the time," she said with a chuckle. "I have my down days like anyone else. Here's the door. I'll hold it. Go inside and turn left. There's an empty booth to your right."

Zac found it without difficulty and slid in. There were huge, colorful pictures, presumably of the menu items offered, above each table. Above theirs was a poster of a turkey dinner.

"That's what I want for lunch," he said, glad the vibrant colors revealed a golden-brown turkey leg, stuffing, corn and a heap of potatoes with gravy dribbling down the sides. "I haven't had a turkey dinner in forever."

"Some places use pressed turkey, not freshly roasted," Abby warned as footsteps moved their way. "You should ask."

Their server poured two fresh mugs of coffee, assured him the turkey was the real thing, noted Abby's order of a Cobb salad without blue cheese and then promised them the apple pie would be out of the oven by the time they were ready for dessert.

Zac tasted his coffee, added another creamer and leaned back in his seat to assess his situation.

"Well?" Abby asked.

"It's better than being blind," he said, understanding exactly what she wanted to know.

"You're disappointed," she murmured, a sadness underlying her words.

"I was." The knot in the back of his neck slowly loosened and dissolved as he peered at her. She wore a green-and-white cardigan over a white blouse. Plain gold hoops hung from her ears. She wore no rings.

"But?"

"But the truth is, I could still be blind. The explosions, the shrapnel, cinders and ash could have completely destroyed my retinas. I guess seeing a little is better than seeing nothing at all." He tilted his head back to stare at her dark head of mussed curls. "You're very beautiful, Abby."

"Now I know your eyesight isn't totally back," she joked. "I'm very ordinary."

"I don't think so." Zac leaned forward. "Will you tell me about your scar?" he asked very quietly.

"Oh!" With a startled gasp, her hand immediately flew to the side of her neck. She touched a spot near her collarbone, then quickly drew her fingers away.

"It's from the accident, isn't it? When Ken and Levi died." She nodded, her fingers tugging her collar tighter as if to hide the knobby marks that lay against her smooth, pale skin. "I'm so sorry."

"It doesn't matter, except that it's a constant reminder that I lost my child," she whispered, sounding bereft and so sad. "And my husband," she added, as if she felt compelled to repeat it to him.

"I doubt you need any reminder of that." He

slid his hand across the table, palm up, and after a glance at his face, she took it. "You've never forgotten a single detail, have you?"

She shook her head, her chin tilted down, face hidden. She stayed that way for a few minutes, probably collecting her composure. Eventually she tugged her hand from his.

"Now that we've covered our disabilities, let's discuss something else." Zac wanted desperately to chase away the sadness and bring a smile to her face.

"Like?" She still didn't look at him.

"Miss P."

"Why?" Abby's head shot up and she stared at him. "Have you thought of anyone suitable for her?"

"You do know I'm not a matchmaker?" he said with a shudder.

"You're not matchmaking. Neither am I." Finally her beautiful smile emerged. "We're just trying to help a friend who is lonely and seeks a companion. What's wrong with that?"

"Nothing, if we could come up with a candidate," Zac said. "I haven't. You?"

"Several gentlemen I met at church seemed suitable," she informed him. "However, when I approached them and brought up her name, they all got this horrified look. Miss Partridge later told me she'd—er—spoken to them en masse."

"Oh, boy." He was afraid to ask. "What did she say to them?"

"Apparently she asked if any of them were interested in a lifetime commitment." When he groaned, Abby argued, "She's a very straightforward person, Zac. She doesn't get the nuances of courtship."

"Nuances, huh? It occurs to me to wonder why you haven't found someone new for yourself." Zac wished he'd never gotten involved in Abby's idea for Miss P. "Maybe we should concentrate on matching you with someone."

"Me?" Her turquoise eyes, which were as amazing as Drew had said, widened. "No. Thank you."

"Why not?" Zac hadn't expected that response, and it made him even more curious about her. "There isn't a man in the world you could possibly find attractive?"

"I'm not—um, interested in a relationship," she offered quietly. "Not right now."

"Meaning not ever?" Zac translated, trying to see her expression more clearly. He paused when the server brought their food, but the moment she left he continued. "You think because your husband was abusive that all men are like him?"

"I'm not that naive, nor am I that foolish," she said with some acerbity, chin thrust out. "I am well aware there are good men in the world. My father was one of them. Abioye's father was another. You and Drew and Ben are three more. My problem with men lies with me. I trusted wrongly before. I'm not going to make that mistake again."

"You'll have to clarify that for me." Zac poked at his turkey leg.

"Something wrong with your meal?" Abby asked, her fork hovering over her salad. Their server was watching him, too.

"Nooo," he drawled, stretching out the vowel. "Just that this leg looks more likely to have come from a dinosaur than a turkey." He tasted a bite. "Nope. Guess it's turkey."

The two ladies giggled before Abby requested more coffee. Then they enjoyed their meals in silence. Abby had long since finished her salad when Zac finally pushed away his half-full plate.

"I can't eat another bite," he told their server, who quickly removed his dishes.

"Wait!" Abby gave the startled woman an apologetic smile. "I'm sorry. I was just wondering if he wanted to take home those bones to show his daughters. It's not every day a kid gets to see dinosaur bones," she said with a smirk.

The woman left laughing. She quickly returned with two pieces of apple pie.

"I can't eat that," Zac protested. But since Abby was already tucking into hers, he decided to give it a shot.

When she pushed away her half-eaten pie and then leaned back with her coffee cup, she voiced the question he'd been avoiding answering.

"Are you feeling more comfortable with counseling now, Zac?"

He finished his dessert slowly, thoughtfully, mulling over the question and then finally nodding.

"Yes?" Her eyes widened.

"I *think* I am. At least, it's begun to feel more natural. Some days I can almost pretend I'm back in Mali, sitting under a baobab tree, talking to fretting patients." He pushed away his plate and leaned back against the seat, trying to understand himself.

"Really?" Abby frowned at him. "Explain, please."

"Maybe it was because I was feeling so comfortable in Peace Meadow. Maybe it was my total blindness. I'm not sure what caused it, but somehow I think I've grown more perceptive to the undercurrents in people's voices, or maybe I sense something in their demeanors. Either way, I can usually discern when the person is desperate for advice, when they only want someone to listen to them or when they realize something is really wrong and actually want help to figure out what that is."

"That's because you're a natural at counseling. You enjoy being with people and hearing their stories. And you care about them," she said confidently. "Those are gifts not everyone has."

"Maybe." Zac didn't really understand what drove his counseling except that he'd always felt moved by the plight of people, even when they asked for help in situations he'd never before dealt with. "It's nothing I ever expected to do," he told her. "But when Leo came, and then that ranch hand Oliver—"

"Never mind all the others who show up at the ranch to talk to you," she inserted with a grin.

"We mostly just talk, you know," he insisted. "That's becoming more comfortable since you began reading those articles and since I've listened to the recordings. I don't feel quite so— what's the word? Outdated? Maybe my little gray cells are recalling my former studies and the work I did."

"That's all great. But who do *you* talk to, Zac?" She studied him as if she was truly interested.

"You." He quickly turned the conversation, blinking to get a clearer view of her face. "You help all of us. Me, Mom and Dad, Drew and Mandy, the twins, Miss Partridge. You're like a one-person support network, Abby."

"Me?" She shook her head while a pink tinge flooded her cheeks. "I don't do anything special."

"You're always doing something. I can feel

your prayers each time I meet with someone," he said. "And I thank you for them." He studied her face and felt forced to admit, "Truthfully? I think your prayers are the reason that, despite my own faith issues, I'm able to recall verses that folks find helpful. God answers your prayers, Abby."

She pushed away her cup and gathered her things.

"I wish He'd answer mine," she mumbled so quietly Zac almost missed it.

"What prayer is that?" he asked.

"The prayer that asks for direction about my future." She waved a hand. "My time with the Calhouns at Hanging Hearts Ranch will be ending now that your sight has begun to return. Soon I'll be moving on. But to what? To where? I have no better idea now than when I first came to this country. Maybe you could pray for me."

As they returned to the car and began the drive home, Zac couldn't get her remarks out of his head. Abby was leaving. He didn't want her to go. In fact, everything in him protested. She made his world make sense when he couldn't. She found solutions when all he saw were problems. The twins loved her dearly. And he…?

Zac was afraid to explore exactly what he felt for this woman who'd swept into his life and brought peace where there'd been none.

Chapter Eleven

With Zac's eyesight partially restored, he finally accepted Drew's offer to help him teach Mia and Zoe to ride. On Sunday afternoon, after a barbecue that followed the Father's Day service at church, Abby sat on the fence to watch the twins' first lesson. She had to stifle her laughter at Mia's unending questions and Zac's patient fatherly responses.

"Does this horsie *want* me to sit on it?" the little girl asked from her perch atop the pony Zac had chosen.

"Yes, sweetie. This horse is named Pixie and she likes to be ridden, but only if you're really nice to her." Zac grimaced at Abby when the little girl bent double and pressed several kisses into Pixie's mane. "Okay, that's enough kissing for now. Remember how I told you to sit?"

"Uh-huh. Does Pixie have a sister?" Mia asked as she straightened.

Abby chuckled when she noted that Drew was having the same difficulty with Zoe who seemed fixated on her lack of cowboy boots.

"They're quite a pair, aren't they?" Bonnie climbed onto the top fence rail beside her.

"Do you mean your sons or the twins?" Abby teased.

"All four. Wait until you meet our other son, Sam." Bonnie sighed. "I hope he comes home soon."

"I hope I'm still here when he does." Abby sensed the older woman's surprise. "It's not that I want to leave," she said quickly. "But Zac's able to see and the doctor said that will improve. Soon he'll have no need for me or my help."

"I think Zac will always have need of you." Bonnie met her surprised stare with a smile. "You two are perfect for each other. You enable Zac to be effective in his work helping others in a way that he barely notices. In talking to people, helping them see their issues more clearly, it's as if he's regained a bit of confidence."

"He is a great listener," Abby agreed. "He refuses to leave anyone immersed in their pain. He coaxes them out of it so well that I believe counseling could be Zac's new ministry. But he only ever talks about going back to medicine."

"Can he?" Bonnie asked frankly.

"That's not for me say." Abby tried to shrug off the pessimism that dogged her spirit today.

"The bandages have been off for weeks now," his mother reminded her.

"I know. He hasn't mentioned that his eyesight has greatly improved, but it may yet." She didn't want to voice any negativism, especially to his mother.

"Sometimes it's very hard to wait for God," Bonnie murmured. "I'd better find Ben. We're supposed to go for a walk." She began walking away.

"Enjoy," Abby called.

Though she watched Zac, Drew and the twins, her thoughts focused on Zac. They'd grown much closer since he'd had his bandages removed, mostly because he'd taken it upon himself to help her fit into ranch life more fully. When she'd goofed up by leaving a pasture gate open, given too much feed to Bonnie's petting animals and made other mistakes, Zac had simply laughed them off.

"It's not funny," she'd insisted, utterly embarrassed. "What if I hurt something?"

"With too much food? Those goats of Mom's loved it. And the cows scared you enough that I'm guessing you'll never leave a pasture gate open again." He'd hooted with laughter when she'd glared at him.

"What about that tack I polished with the wrong stuff?" she demanded.

"It looks better than it did before, according to Mandy." Zac never raised his voice, never made her feel stupid or klutzy. Mostly he just teased her about her mistakes and she liked that. A lot.

With Zac, Abby felt valued, appreciated and, best of all, included as a competent, capable adult, something she'd never felt with Ken. The past two nights as she and Zac had sat on the deck admiring the stars, he'd somehow coaxed her to reveal things about her failed marriage that she'd never told anyone else. What he'd said after that still confounded her.

You know, I wonder if Ken may have suffered abuse in his own past. Perhaps he didn't know how to deal with it. Perhaps all he knew was to carry on what he'd learned.

The comment was shocking to Abby, and yet the more she considered the possibility, the easier it became to release some of the blame she still carried for what she believed was her failure at marriage. Ken didn't have any parents when she'd met him, but maybe he'd grown up in abusive situations and never knew anything different.

"Did you see me, Abby?" Mia wanted to know, free of her horse now and swinging her dad's hand. "I rided a horsie."

"You sure did. And very well, too." Abby embraced the delightful little girl and then repeated her praise when Zoe joined them. "If they have horses at the day camp you two are going to attend soon, you'll both do very well." She'd said it deliberately to remind Zac that she was determined the girls should get more involved with kids their own age.

Judging by his intense scrutiny, he knew exactly what she was up to. She ducked her head, a little embarrassed by her own audacity but determined to stand up for her decision, if need be.

Bu there was no need. Zac didn't argue.

"We're going to see the kittens in the barn now," he explained, a battered gray Stetson tilted back on his head. "Wanna come?"

"It's Dad's Day. You go with your daughters. I'm going to sit here and enjoy the sun." She watched them leave with a bittersweet longing.

She loved looking at Zac, loved the way his hair flopped over one twinkling eye, just visible through his dark glasses. She loved the way he always brushed it and other distractions off to focus on whomever he was talking to. She loved…

Wait a minute—*loved*?

Yes, Abby acknowledged to herself, astonished and yet overjoyed by the thought. She loved Zac. He was such a decent, honorable man. Being here on the ranch, being near Zac, watching him interact with his beloved family, enjoying their moments together—all of that only enhanced her budding feelings for this man who still struggled to trust God. Here at the Double H Ranch she'd found freedom, especially because of Zac's unconditional acceptance of her.

But Abby was still tortured by reminders of Ken's about-face after he'd learned of the insurance. She'd loved her husband. She'd thought he loved her. But she'd been fooled. Ken had only loved what she could do for him. So even if Zac was interested in her, and she wasn't at all sure he was, Abby was afraid to risk love again. Even for a man who was as special as Zac Calhoun.

And yet, Abby had witnessed great marriages during her stay at Hanging Hearts Ranch. Zac's parents, Drew and Mandy and several local church couples exemplified unions with mutual respect and mutual goals, marriage the way God intended.

"Why are you sitting here?" Miss Partridge asked, breaking into her reverie.

"Hello. The girls were learning to ride and I watched," Abby explained, slightly embarrassed that she hadn't even heard the woman's approach. "I stayed put to enjoy the sunshine. How are you?"

"Wishing you and Zac would find me someone. There's a cruise to Alaska I really want to take." She grimaced. "But it's no fun to go alone."

"No, that wouldn't be nearly as interesting," Abby agreed as she climbed down off the fence. "Would you like some coffee?"

"I'd rather go sit in Peace Meadow and talk to you." Miss Partridge wore a determined look on her face that said she would not be swayed.

"Sure. Let's go." Uncertain as to what this was about, Abby waited until they were sitting in the meadow before she opened her mouth. Miss Partridge beat her to it.

"I hear you're leaving."

"What?" Startled, she gaped at the older woman. "Who said that? Well, I mean I *will* be leaving soon now that Zac's recovered partial sight, but not for a bit..."

"I'm really disappointed to hear that." Miss Partridge thrust out her legs and peered at her walking shoes. "Extremely disappointed."

"Really?" Abby blinked. "But, Miss P., you know that I always intended to leave when he regained his sight."

"You're leaving even though you love him?" The woman's clear blue eyes dared her to refute it.

Embarrassed and in shock, Abby remained silent, staring at her knotted fingers. Why had she come to the meadow? Now that she was virtually alone with Miss P., there would be no stopping her questioning and probing.

"You don't have to worry. I doubt anyone else realizes the depth of your feelings for Zac." Had she ever heard this woman sound so tender, so loving? "I noticed because I've seen how changed you are around him. I've been praying for Zachary to find another partner since the day Bonnie told me Maria had died."

"You have? Why?" Abby asked curiously.

"Because I pray for all the Calhoun boys," she explained with a shrug. "I felt like we all—the entire town of Sunshine—adopted them after their birth parents were killed in that car accident and Ben and Bonnie brought them to Hanging Hearts Ranch. I've watched and prayed over them through school and beyond, like an aunt. Because the three of them are special men and I believe God has plans to use them."

"That's wonderful that you're so committed to them." Admiration swept over Abby. "I once had an African woman, a very dear friend, who prayed for me. Her prayers were the reason I got through—" She choked up and couldn't actually finish.

"She got you through the abuse from your husband." Miss P. nodded. "It must have been wonderful to know that you had someone holding you up before God when things were at their worst."

"How did you know about the…abuse?" she asked, aghast.

"The way you never spoke of your husband without a tenseness in your voice and your body language. Little things I've seen, like the way you used to shy away from touch." Miss P. smiled and shrugged. "I spent a week of my yearly holidays from the library helping out at a women's shelter in the city. You learn to recognize when a woman has been abused. Mental abuse is, I often think, the most difficult to recover from. Bodies heal, but once damaged, self-confidence is very hard to rebuild. I'm guessing that's what you endured. But you seem to be regaining yours since you've come to the Double H."

"Maybe, but I still feel guilty for not making it work with Ken," Abby murmured. "I tried to be what he needed, but there were barriers between us that I couldn't break down."

"Your insurance money," the senior said with a nod.

"How do you—?"

"I did an online search and found out some things. Librarians know how to search," she said with a smug smile. "I didn't want to poke into your personal life, dear. I just wanted to protect my boys."

Her boys. Never had Abby heard such pride as she did in this woman's voice.

"So you know all about me?" she whispered, wincing inwardly.

"I know your parents died and you received a settlement because of the way they died. A crooked politician, wasn't it? Trying to cover up his drunk driving?" She shook her head. "Be sure your sin will find you out, the Bible says."

"His didn't," Abby muttered.

"It will." Miss P.'s jaw thrust out. "I also read that you'd lost your little son and Ken in a horrific accident. I'm so sorry, Abby. That's such a difficult loss." Long fingers gripped her hand and squeezed sympathetically.

"Thank you. Ken took a lot of chances when he flew. That day he was so angry with me that he took too many." She shook off the memories.

"But Zac is nothing like your husband was. Zac wouldn't hurt anyone knowingly," Miss P. insisted.

"I know that. Zac doesn't have a desperate need to prove himself. He's giving and kind, always ready to listen. He doesn't have a self-centered bone in his body."

"But you don't want to give him a chance?" Miss P. interjected with her brows drawn together as if she couldn't understand that.

"Let's say once burned, twice shy." Abby heaved a heavy sigh, wondering why it was so easy to talk to this friend. "I'm scared to trust myself when it comes to love. I'm scared I'll fail again. I loved Ken, but I don't believe he loved me. That was pretense."

"His pretense," the lady said indignantly. "Not yours."

"Yes, but still, I loved the wrong man. That love made me weak and my weakness cost me Levi." She burst into hot, hurting tears. "I can't risk loving and losing again. It would kill me."

"No, dear. You are strong, much stronger than you think." Miss P. crouched beside her chair, her arm around Abby's shoulders. "And you have God on your side, loving you, supporting you. Protecting you. Preparing a future for you."

"My future isn't with Zac or the twins," Abby whispered. "Not at Hanging Hearts Ranch."

"Why do you think that?" Miss P. stared at the horizon as if mesmerized.

"Because if we did get involved and I messed up, it would hurt so many people, especially the twins. How would they ever understand if I left? They wouldn't. They'd just have to deal with another loss." She gulped. "His parents would be shamed in the community they love. Mandy and Drew and Ella would all have their lives disrupted." She swallowed hard. "It couldn't work."

"Do you want it to?" her friend demanded.

"Yes," Abby admitted. "But that's not the most important consideration."

"Yes, dear, it is. It is the *only* consideration.

Do you know how much I long to find love, to share love, to be loved?" Tears pooled as Miss P. smiled. "Love is God's greatest gift. Love can work wonders, in us and around us. My dear, with God all things are possible."

"But—"

"Why don't you and I spend some time here talking to Him about you and Zac," Miss P. suggested. "I'm sure He's already got a plan for both of you to share His blessings."

"Zac doesn't love me," Abby insisted.

A very odd smile stretched across Miss Partridge's face. Then the lady bowed her head and began talking to God.

Meet me in Peace Meadow.

Zac was rather perplexed by the text. Abby had disappeared for most of the afternoon, which he and the twins had spent with Ben. Now his mom and dad had gone to a seniors' dinner in town. Since Mandy and Ella were taking Drew out for a Father's Day dinner, Zac needed to fetch his twins and think about what to make them for supper.

Where had his nurse been this afternoon?

The twins are with me, a second text declared.

"What on earth is going on?" Zac wasted a few minutes puzzling over it before deciding he might as well find out. He shrugged into a sweater, walked down the steps and grabbed the end of the rope that would lead him to Peace Meadow. He could see well enough without it, but the uneven ground sometimes tripped him up. Abby's knots in the rope helped with that.

It wouldn't get dark for hours yet, but the waning sun created leafy patterns on the ground where it shone through the leaves. Zac peered through his glasses, recognizing the outlines of buildings around the ranch. Would his eyesight ever get clearer, or was this blurry-around-the-edges view the best he could hope for?

And if it was, what kind of a future could he have? The mission society wouldn't want to re-sponsor him, especially with diminished sight, when they'd barely agreed to him staying after Maria's death. So what would he do? And where would he do it?

Zac couldn't figure that out. But neither could he imagine a future that didn't include Abby. Her earlier remark about leaving had stuck with him, rolling around and around in his head, reminding him he'd soon be on his own. Life without Abby would be very different. She was the type of person he called a cheerleader, always there with an encouraging word, teaching the girls through her actions how to be kind.

Abby intuitively saw needs others missed and

stepped in to fill them. Now that his parents were healing and past the critical stage, outside help from the community had waned, probably at their insistence. It was Abby who checked that his mom and dad had nutritious meals ready to eat when they were too tired or sore to cook. It was Abby who, with Miss Partridge's help, had organized the church ladies to take over the spring housecleaning because his mom couldn't manage it. It was Abby who nudged Zac to make it more of a habit to stop by his parents' home at different times each day, just to visit or share a coffee or chat.

No matter what her task, Abby always wore her uplifting smile that cheered everyone just by its very appearance. What would his life be like without her gorgeous grin?

He learned more about Abby every day. Today, for instance, he'd heard her playing his father's favorite hymn on his parents' piano. He had no idea she could play, let alone sing, and yet her voice was amazing. To Zac, it seemed the only thing Abby couldn't do was find Miss Partridge someone to love.

Because he wasn't concentrating on where he was going, Zac suddenly found himself in the meadow, assailed by two squeaky voices wishing him a happy Father's Day. Zoe and Mia grinned with delight while he gaped at the array before him.

"Thank you, girls. That was very nice." He received their enthusiastic hugs and kisses, then glanced at Abby. "What's going on?"

"We're having a wiener roast, Daddy," Zoe proclaimed.

"For your Daddy's Day party." Mia joined her sister in dancing around him with excitement. "An' we got presents an'—ow!" She looked at her sister angrily.

"Not s'posed to tell, dummy," Zoe said.

"Girls. That's not the way we act, on Father's Day or any other time," Abby admonished very quietly.

"Sorry, Daddy," the twins said together with sad faces, then ruined their contrition by giggling.

"A nice party from my beautiful twins. Thank you. And Abby lit a fire?" Zac studied her. "Is there no end to your talents?"

"I'll have you know I lit a fire in my African stove almost every day, Zachary," Abby chided briskly. "It's hardly a talent."

"For some people it is. Ask Mandy." He sat down in the chair the twins indicated, the one with colorful balloons tied to the back that bobbled in the wind. "What now? Oh." He leaned over to allow them to put a paper crown on his head. "Let the party begin," he declared, thrilled that she'd gone to all this work and engaged the girls in it, just for him.

"We're cookin' your supper tonight, Daddy," Zoe informed him.

"Yeah. Cookin'. Oops." Mia peered sadly at the hot dog that had just fallen into the fire.

"Let's try that again," Abby said cheerfully, and threaded a second wiener onto Mia's long cooking fork.

"Abby calls that a do-over, Daddy," Zoe explained in typical big-sister form.

"They're just so cute," Abby said almost under her breath as she sat down beside him.

"They take after their father," he informed her smugly.

"Hmm." She appraised him thoughtfully as the warm breeze whispered across the meadow.

Zac found he couldn't look away from her. What was it about Abby that captivated him?

"Well, you're cute," she murmured, her smile playful. "And you're their father, so I guess they do take after you."

She thought he was cute, huh? Even with bad eyes and these dark glasses? A quiet sense of satisfaction settled inside him. Once the hot dogs had been devoured, Zac pretended to rise.

"Guess we'd better get going home."

"No, Daddy!" Zoe yelled, seizing his hands and hanging on. "Wait."

"Wait? Why?" He pretended to frown.

"'Cause we got 'nother s'prise," Mia explained.

"Another? Well, what could that be?" He sat down and managed to look suitably impressed when they opened a big plastic carrier and lifted out a large flat cake.

"It's choc'late, like you like best," Zoe explained.

"It looks delish." He tipped his head to study them. "You girls made it? For me?"

"Uh-huh." Zoe grinned. "An' Abby helped."

"When did you do this?" he asked, directing his question at Abby.

"Yesterday, when you were here, talking to that man." Mia used a plastic knife to cut a huge piece. "This is mine."

Abby cleared her throat.

Mia hesitated before revising.

"It's my piece for Daddy, 'cause it's Daddy's Day an' at Sunday School Teacher tol' us we're s'posed to be nice to you."

"Didn't she say you're supposed to be nice to me all the time?" Zac asked innocently.

"Yeah." Zoe shrugged. "We'll try."

Zac noticed Abby turn away to cough. He had to fight to keep a straight face, too. They enjoyed their cake and when it was gone, Abby gave them each a balsa wood plane to fly. Hers crashed first. Zac deliberately sent his to the same fate so the girls could keep playing while he and Abby talked.

"Thank you. For everything. This was very thoughtful of you to arrange." He sat next to her.

"I used to do stuff like this with my dad on Father's Day. Fun things like flying little planes or kites I gave him. I miss him." For a moment, a wistful expression fluttered through her incredible eyes, dimming them.

"And with Ken," he added, not wanting to dwell on that image.

"No, Ken was away—" She stopped short, voice quavering. After a moment she began again. "Levi just had one Father's Day, but his daddy wasn't there. He was flying." She shook her head as tears coursed down her lovely face.

"I'm so sorry, Abby." He covered her hand with his, silently sympathizing as he waited for her to regain her composure. Her strong capable fingers rested in his, reminding him of her strength and how seldom she let anyone see any weakness beneath her mantle of capability. This woman gave and gave, but rarely asked or even looked as if she needed comforting.

"Daddy?"

"Yes, Zoe?" Zac blinked, surprised to realize both his daughters were staring at his hand on Abby's.

"How come you're holding Abby's hand? Are you gonna kiss her, too?" Mia asked curiously.

"What? I don't—who said—why are you asking this?" he demanded, yanking his hand away.

"'Cause Ella said that's how her mom and dad got married. First they hanged on to the other person's hand and then they kissed," Mia said.

"An' then they got married." Zoe's eyes glowed with excitement. "Are you an' Abby getting married? Is she gonna be our mom?"

Surprised by the intense appeal of their idea, Zac glanced at Abby, who now stared at the twins as if they'd dropped from Mars. After a moment her head swiveled and she looked at him, her beautiful eyes stretched wide.

That's when Zac knew he did want to kiss her. Thoroughly. But not here, and certainly not with the twins watching.

"Wait till I tell Ella," Mia yelled enthusiastically, hopping from one foot to the other.

"An' the kids at Sunday school." Zoe and her sister shared huge grins.

"Wait! Girls." It was up to him to clear this up and he knew it. Problem was, for the life of him Zac couldn't figure out how to tell them there wasn't going to be a wedding. He'd destroy their excitement and maybe even ruin this Father's Day surprise they'd arranged. He couldn't do that.

But wasn't it funny how absolutely certain Zac was that marriage to Abby could never be a mistake?

Chapter Twelve

"So you're getting married?" Miss Partridge clomped up the deck stairs energetically. "I thought since we're friends, you might have told me first."

"Married?" Abby dropped her mending to stare. "Who told you that?" She had a sneaking suspicion she already knew the answer, but her friend's response wasn't what she expected.

"It's all over town. It was the first thing the twins announced at their day camp this morning." Miss Partridge peered at her fingernails as if they were of immense interest as she recited, "You and Zac were kissing in Peace Meadow. Now you're getting married. So when's the big day?"

"There isn't one," Abby said firmly, though inside she mourned saying the words. "I am not getting married. To anyone."

"But…?" Her friend leaned back, obviously waiting to hear the story.

"The twins and I made a Father's Day celebration for Zac in the meadow. He and I were talking while the girls played. I was talking about Ken," she added meaningfully.

"Ah." Miss Partridge nodded. "Go on."

"I started bawling and he was trying to comfort me." Abby's face grew hot with embarrassment. "The girls saw it and thanks to something Ella had told them, mistook our joined hands as a prelude for upcoming nuptials."

"Rats!"

Abby gaped at the older woman, totally disconcerted by the huge grin she wore. "Sorry?"

"I was really hoping the two of you would get together without a nudge from me." Miss P. sighed. "I guess not. Okay, then."

"Miss Partridge—Grace. Please don't do anything. Zac and I aren't going to get together. He doesn't love me, and anyway—" Abby knew she was going to have to come up with a strong reason to stop this determined woman from meddling. "I'm not sure I want to give up my plans to travel and stay here, with him."

"What?" Miss P. reared back in astonishment. "But you said—"

"I made a mistake. I got caught up in the idea. I mistook the thrill of being here—in this wonderful place with Zac, who is like no one I've ever met—as something more than just friendship. But it isn't." Abby met her searching stare. "We're not getting married."

"Huh." Miss Partridge slumped in her chair. "I was so hopeful…" She let that go and glanced around. "Where is Zac?"

"With Bonnie. She told him about two ladies who have issues trusting horses, thinking Zac might be able to help them." Abby smiled. "Then he'll be busy preparing a talk to give at that men's thing at the church tonight."

"He agreed to do that? But the pastor said he'd completely shot down the idea of public speaking." The lady looked shocked. "Last I heard, the men were hosting some visiting salesman."

"Apparently he canceled. Drew asked Zac, and when he refused, Drew insisted on a dart challenge. Zac lost so he has to give the talk." She shrugged. "I don't know the details, but Drew was gloating and Zac didn't seem too upset by it."

"As boys, they used to compete in a dart throw to settle their arguments." Miss P. frowned. "Zac has an excellent shot. I'm surprised Drew won."

"Well, he did." Abby shrugged. "Zac won't do anything formal, just an off-the-cuff talk about his life in Africa. I think he's going to record it so Melanie can hear." She put her mending to one side. It was so much more interesting to talk with her friend. "Do you need to see him?"

"Not necessarily." Miss Partridge made a show of peering into the distance. "He mentioned at church that he had something he wanted to share with me so I came to find out what."

"Do you want me to call him?" She didn't like the librarian's glum expression.

"No, thanks." Miss Partridge's scrutiny intensified. "He said he might know someone," she finally blurted.

"Someone…? Oh." The truth dawned. "Someone special for you. I'm sorry, I don't know who that might be, but I will tell Zac you stopped by," she promised.

"You know, it's odd that you suddenly decided you don't want to stay here." Miss Partridge's eyes narrowed. "Tell me again why that's changed."

"It's not a change so much as a realization." Abby decided to be completely honest. "For one thing, even if Zac did care about me, I might fail him, as I failed my husband."

"More like *your husband* failed you!" The woman gave a unladylike snort.

"Maybe we failed each other. Anyway, I've stopped trying to figure it out." Abby shook her head. "I'll probably never know why God didn't protect me from Ken's betrayal any more than

Zac will learn why God allowed someone to destroy his life's work. And even if I knew, what can I do about it? I must move on."

"You're focusing on the future," the lady murmured.

"Yes. I'll always miss Levi, but I can't keep mourning him. He's safe with God. In Africa I buried myself in caring for needy kids so I wouldn't be alone, so I didn't have to think about having no one. Then the government closed down my orphanage. I came here to start over. It's time for me to really live, to face my future, though I'm not exactly sure how to do that," she admitted. "I want a full, happy life, but where do I start?"

"You've already started. Here, with this family." Miss P. leaned forward and placed her hand over Abby's. "You're not alone. The twins adore you. Ben and Bonnie think you're fantastic. Drew and Mandy keep singing your praises. Zac depends on you to keep things going for him and build his spirits." She squinted. "You know, maybe you and I could come up with something you can do on the Double H, so you won't have to leave."

"Like what? Nursing?" Abby chuckled. "Everyone here is too healthy." She looked at the sky, hoping for some revelation. "I greatly admire Zac's spirit. He's slowly taking what he's been dealt and working it through. It isn't easy for him, but he doesn't give up. I won't, either. God has a purpose for me. I just have to find it."

"That's the spirit, my dear." Miss P. hugged her, headed for the stairs but then stopped. "Oh. I almost forgot. I came to invite you for dinner. I'd like us to celebrate our friendship over a meal. Would two weeks from Saturday work?"

"Thank you, I'd love to, though I'll have to check with Zac."

"Do that, but don't mention the dinner. I don't want him to be jealous." With a coy smile, Miss P. waved, then descended the stairs. "Bye."

As Abby watched her leave in a cloud of dust, something about the woman's hasty departure niggled at her brain. But the more she puzzled over it, the less she could determine why it bothered her. When Zac returned and invited her for a walk, all thoughts of Grace Partridge fled.

She strolled beside him, toward the meadow, of course. They always seemed to gravitate there. Only now he moved more confidently. He was regaining his self-confidence and she was so glad about that.

"Uneasy about your talk tonight?"

"Of course. Who am I, with all my questions about God, to be talking about faith and trust?" He shoved his dark glasses up onto his nose with a grimace. "I'm hardly a sterling example of faith, Abby."

"Having questions isn't a sin," she scolded with a smile.

"No, but mine are so many that I feel I've lost my connection with God." His fingers found the back of the chair and he sank into it. "I'm so tired of feeling betrayed and confused and uncertain."

"Then stop." Abby sat down beside him.

"Great idea." He shot her a mocking look. "How?"

"Fight it. Refuse to indulge in those thoughts," she said firmly. "God loves you, Zac. Whether you choose to believe it or not has no relevance. He does. You can't change that love or make it fit the way you want. You either believe in His love or you don't. And if you believe it, and I think you do," she said with a quick smile of reassurance, "then all your fretting and fussing and trying to make God answer to you is useless. God is God. He knows what He's doing, whether you trust that or not."

"You don't mince words, do you, Abby?" Though he studied her, she found it impossible to gauge his reaction to her comments because of the darkened tinted lenses that shielded his eyes. "You're saying I should accept God, period. Don't expect Him to answer to me. Give up everything I've believed about Him since I was seven?"

"Maybe your childhood beliefs about God need to grow, change. Deep inside you know the truth of what I'm saying." She squirmed uncomfortably under his continued stare, but she had to finish her thought. "Doesn't it all boil down to the basic tenet of trust in God? All the way or not at all."

He was quiet for a long time. She didn't interrupt, content to let God do His work.

"'Blessed are the pure in heart for they shall see God,'" Zac quoted softly. "That's you, Abby. You have this sweet, genuine trust that God will work out everything."

"You make me sound gullible." Her face warmed. "I'm not some silly Goody Two-shoes. I've had lots of faith issues to work out. I'm still working on some. But I believe the Bible when it says all things work together for good for those who are called by God, according to *His* purpose."

"You're okay with whatever He decides?" His lips thinned.

"Yes, Zac." She slid her hand into his. "I'm okay with letting God be God, because as His beloved child, I trust that His purpose is what's best for me."

After speaking at the men's dinner, Zac was invited to give presentations at three different events in three different counties, all in the same week. At the end of each talk, people sought him out to ask if they could meet with him privately. He agreed and set up appointments simply because he couldn't turn them away, but also because Abby's words lingered in his brain. Was this some kind of new ministry for him?

The days flew past as folks came to the ranch. In the solace of Peace Meadow, over Abby's carefully prepared snacks and cool drinks, each one poured out their pain and anguish, desperate for help, as if Zac had answers for years of parental neglect, for a spouse's unfaithfulness, for a beloved child's betrayal, for a friend's damaging gossip. He didn't, but somehow the words came to him, mingled with verses that seemed to bring relief to their battered hearts.

On Friday night, bemused and wearied by the sheer numbers who had shown up, Zac asked Bonnie to babysit while he unburdened his heart to Abby in Peace Meadow.

"It's so strange," he confessed. "I personally have no answers to their problems. But they talk and a verse springs to mind. When I say it, it's like a light switch flicks and God is illuminated instead of their problems."

"So God's using you to heal hearts and souls, just as we ask Him to do each morning after breakfast." She smiled at him as if he'd done something wonderful. "What's the problem?"

"Me. I don't have anything special to tell them," he argued, feeling totally at a loss. "I don't have the answers they seek."

"You don't need to. You know God, Zac. You've known him since you were seven. He hasn't changed." Her palm against his cheek, then touching his chest, left a trail of warmth glowing inside him. "You just have to remind them that God's their Father and He's there, holding those verses you memorized so long ago because He knew you'd need them for yourself and for the people who look to you. He's drawing them to Himself through you because He's the only one who can comfort their hurting hearts. He who was, who is and who always will be our Father."

"Sometimes it's very hard to hear their stories." He loved that Abby came, listened, stayed and always drew him back to God. If he really was ministering, then she was partnering with her constant, steady support. "These are people living confused lives. They're in desperate pain. They make my issues seem small. That's why I can't send them away."

"And that's why you're so successful, my dear, dear man." Abby's hand squeezed his, her touch like a blessing.

"But I don't feel genuine. I still have questions. I still can't wholly trust God," he reminded her. "I still need answers, Abby."

"The apostle Peter questioned why God didn't take away his affliction," she reminded.

"He asked for healing, three times," Zac reminded her.

"And he said God didn't heal him. How frustrating that must have been when he was suffering so much to spread God's love. But this affliction didn't stop Paul from his ministry," she reminded. "He kept going. He had perseverance and dedication. So do you. That's what makes a missionary a missionary."

"But I'm not a missionary. Not anymore." It didn't seem as hard to admit that as it had been.

"Yes, Zac. You are." The intensity of Abby's voice held him captive. "A missionary isn't just one who leaves his homeland for a foreign country. A missionary is one who ministers no matter where he is. There are mission fields in the most unlikely places, even here in Montana. Perhaps Peace Meadow at Hanging Hearts Ranch is your new mission."

She drew her hand away, leaving Zac reeling at the loss of her tender touch. It was all so confusing, and now eyestrain had given him a pounding headache. He rubbed his temples.

"Your head hurts." She rose, moved behind him and soothed the knot in his neck. "Better?" she asked before she sat down again.

"Yes, thank you." What would he do without

her? She'd slipped into his world and given him hope, and he doubted she realized how great a gift that was.

"Zac? I need to tell you something."

"Okay." He held his breath, worried.

"I think I'll be moving on after next week," she said in a rush. "You don't really need me here anymore. Actually, you probably never did need me. But I'm so glad I came." The smile lighting up her face revealed a joy he envied. "You're seeing now. You can get around. You can administer your own eye treatment. The girls are comfortable here. They'll be okay with a nanny to watch them. There's not really much more for me to do."

"There is a lot for you to do," he argued as his stomach sank to his toes. "Every day you teach the girls things their mother would have taught them. You pray for us, especially this new work I'm doing. You lead all of us by your strong faith example. My parents love having you here."

"But they don't *need* me," she said with a hint of sadness. "No one does."

I do. The thought shocked him into silence.

"You're all getting on with your lives. I'm glad. That's exactly the way it should be." Her smile, her beautiful smile. What if he never saw it again? "I need to get on with my life, with finding my place and discovering where God wants me."

Here. You belong here. With me.

"I want you to know that wherever I go, whatever I do, I won't forget Hanging Hearts Ranch or the ones who live here. You're all in my heart now and I will continue to pray for everyone, especially you," she added. "I'll pray that you will learn to truly trust God with all your heart. Because there's no other way to be happy except to trust and obey."

A text from Bonnie saying Mia was calling for her made Abby jump to her feet. After ascertaining there was nothing wrong, Zac urged her to go and leave him to find his own way back. He claimed he wanted to think for a while, but the truth was he couldn't shake her words.

Abby was leaving. Their long walks and never ending discussions about life, God and learning His ways would be over in a little more than a week. He would be alone. Again.

Why did it feel like he was about to lose his left arm?

Because you love her.

That still, small voice inside gutted him with the truth. He did love Abby. He loved her beauty, internal and external. He loved the care and attention she showered on everyone she came in contact with. Even strangers who arrived to talk with Zac were welcomed with freshly baked cookies and a cool beverage. People with whom she had no relationship, and yet she made their lives better just by being available, by caring however she was able.

Even aloof Miss Partridge had found a soul mate in Abby. Why? Because Abby saw past the lady's pretense of self-dependence to the aching heart beneath. She cared so much she was willing to help Miss P. achieve her dream of love.

Zac loved Abby.

I love her. He tested the words in his mind and reveled in a deep satisfaction. Abby belonged here, with him. He wanted her to stay permanently, to help him figure out this new path he was on, to be the voice of reason and truth in his world, to keep pointing him back to God.

But what had he, a jobless, half-sighted man with no future, to offer a woman as beautiful both inside and out as Abby?

"God? Can't You do something?" he pleaded. And then he voiced his deepest fear. "Are You taking her away from me, too?"

Loath to leave this place that now seemed like home, Abby spent as much time as she could with the dear ones at Hanging Hearts Ranch. She'd grown to love each as if they were her own family. The girls' bubbling laughter helped change her memories of Levi to joyful recollections that honored his memory. She rested in the knowledge that she would see him again one day, but until then, God cared for her son. Time with Zac had healed her heart from Ken's abuse, too, allowing her to finally and irrevocably turn her mistakes over to God.

Though her heart ached with longing, though she yearned to stay, to see the girls grow and change, to watch Zac blossom in the ministry for which he was made, Abby shed her tears in private with God as her witness, determined that no one would remember her crying.

When she'd told Miss Partridge of her plan to leave the day after their farewell dinner, the woman had begged a favor.

"Bonnie said you're an amazing pianist and vocalist, yet we've never heard you at church. Will you please give us a special treat before you leave? Choose any song you like."

After some persuading, Abby had agreed, though she was nervous about it. She would sing her mother's favorite song as a tribute to God.

So on her last Sunday morning, with the entire congregation watching, she walked to the piano, seated herself and took a deep breath. Then she closed her eyes and began quietly playing the introduction to a song written long ago, but as relevant today as it ever had been.

"Oh love that will not let me go, I rest my weary soul in thee.

"I give thee back the life I owe, that in thine ocean depths its flow.

"May richer, fuller be."

The moving words and eerie melody combined to echo through the silent sanctuary, but Abby was utterly focused on the message. Would Zac understand this next verse, know that she sang it especially for him? Would he finally realize that leaving him was the hardest thing she'd ever have to do?

"Oh Joy that seekest me through pain, I cannot close my heart to Thee,

"I trace the rainbow through the rain, And feel the promise is not vain..."

She sang on, using the last verse as her own promise to God. As she did, sweet peace filled her. It would be painful to leave the ranch, Zoe and Mia and especially Zac. But God would see her through.

Abby let the final evocative notes die away before she rose and walked to her pew, head bent, not quite able to meet Zac's gaze. Suddenly, applause filled the room. It was disconcerting yet somehow richly fulfilling to hear that others felt the same resonance in those words that she had. Zac was applauding, too, though he wore a brooding look, as if the song troubled him.

"Those words," he said as she drove back to the ranch after the service. "They're deep."

"Isn't it amazing that Matheson, the man who wrote them, is said to have penned the hymn in only five minutes during a time of distress?" She glanced at him. "I agreed with the pastor today when he said problems force us to figure out what we really believe."

"Huh." He said little more as they rode home, apparently deep in thought.

Abby prepared a picnic lunch to enjoy in the meadow. Zoe and Mia skipped along at her side. Zac walked by the rope she'd strung, though lately he'd stopped hanging on. Perhaps he used it as a visual cue. Abby didn't know if that was because his sight was improving or out of sheer determination to be independent, and she didn't care. It was enough just to spend time with him and the girls, to share the beautiful meadow.

"I love summer, with those lovely mountains looming over us and everything so green," she said after finishing her sandwich. "God makes such beautiful things."

"Hard to believe that three years ago so much of this land was black and ugly from forest fires," Zac said. "Reminds me of a verse. 'To give them beauty for ashes, the oil of joy for mourning, the garment of praise for the spirit of heaviness,'" he recited.

"That verse perfectly describes how God

changes us from weaklings to strong trees. He exchanges our negatives for positives."

She got caught in Zac's stare, felt the intensity of it to her marrow. How sad that this wonderful man didn't realize how deeply bound he was by God's love.

"Daddy?" Zoe snuggled beside Zac and leaned her head against his arm as if she was very weary. "Why does Abby have to go away?"

Abby's sprit groaned. She'd informed the twins of her plans two days ago and endured a barrage of questions and bursts of tears ever since. She hated causing them pain, but she couldn't stay at Hanging Hearts forever.

"Yeah, why?" Mia repeated, taking her place on his other knee. "Last night we asked you why Mommy died an' you said families grow and change, an'—"

"Our family changed when you gotted your eyes hurt and Abby looked after us," Zoe butted in, not to be outdone by her sister. "Now Abby's part of our family, isn't she?"

"She is." Mia nodded enthusiastically. "'Cause she keeped staying here with us," she said, brown eyes glowing with wisdom.

"When we comed here we got more family." Zoe counted them off on her fingers. "A grandma and a grandpa an' a uncle, an' a aunt an' a cousin."

"Yeah," Mia agreed. "So me an' Zoe were wonderin' why we can't get another mom? An Abby mom."

"Not 'cause we didn't love our other mom," Zoe quickly added. "But we need a mom now. Me an' Mia prayed and prayed an' we think God gived us Abby to be our new mom."

"Yeah." Mia stared at her father with anticipation. "Okay?"

Zac looked like he'd been hit with a snowball. The girls waited patiently for a few minutes, but when he didn't answer they began wiggling, growing excited about the prospect of having a new mom. Abby had to step in.

"My dear, dear girls," she began, struggling to speak past her sudden hoarseness. "I love you both very much and there is nothing I would like more than to be your mom. But I can't," she inserted quickly, before they could start celebrating.

"How come?" Zoe demanded.

"Did we do sumthin' bad?" Mia asked sadly, tears shimmering, ready to tumble down her face. "'Cause we're sorry if we did."

"You didn't do anything bad, darling. You've been loving and kind and generous. I've had so much fun with you."

"Then how come—"

She couldn't let their hopes build, though she hated dashing them.

"Things change. People change. Families change, just like your dad said," she offered quietly, her heart breaking. She dare not look at Zac or she would break down. "I was part of your family for a special few months and it was so wonderful. But you and your dad live here. I have to go find my own home. I don't belong here. But you do. You and your dad and your grandparents and Ella and her parents. You all belong together. Because you're a family. Do you understand?"

"No." Zoe stuck out her bottom lip in a pout. "Daddy told that man who came here yesterday that families can be lots of different people. Right, Daddy?"

"You did," Mia reminded Zac before he could answer.

"They can," Abby agreed. "If they want to."

"You don't want to be in our family?" Zoe and Mia wore identical frowns.

"It's not that I don't want to," Abby rushed to reassure these precious twins. "I just…can't." She couldn't do this anymore. She jumped up and walked away as her heart broke, releasing sad tears.

"I think we shouldn't talk about this anymore, girls. Okay?" Zac's quiet voice reached Abby, his voice gentle, reassuring. "We don't want to make Abby sad, do we?"

"No!" The twins were unanimous.

"We love Abby," Zoe insisted.

"Yeah, we love her." Sweet Mia always got the last word.

Abby kept walking away from them as she begged God to heal her heart. How wonderful it would be to stay, to be part of this family, to love and be loved. *I yield my flickering torch to thee.* The words from her solo reminded her that God was in control. That whatever happened, He would be there.

But oh, how she wished she didn't have to go.

The following week was torture for Zac. He couldn't get the twins' question out of his head. They prompted visions of a future that he longed for but was afraid to entertain.

Abby as part of their family? Abby staying here, helping wherever she was needed, brightening every day with her sweet smile, sharing his hopes and fears? Coming to him with her worries, allowing him to comfort her, protect her. Love her.

Life without Abby. That thought was terrifying. Why?

Because she belonged here. She belonged with him. She was not a stranger. She was part of every facet of his life. He'd taken her for granted. Who, other than Abby, could he trust to love the twins as much as he did? He loved so many things about her. Her selfless generosity in fixing up the meadow so he could go there. Her unstinting help with his parents and around the ranch. Even her insistence that they help find Miss P. a boyfriend.

Friday evening Zac sat in the meadow, mulling it all over. His lips curved as he recalled the utter fiasco of his latest attempt at matchmaking. Miss Partridge and Arthur Mendel were so not the combination he'd hoped for. Abby had warned him on Monday.

"Arthur isn't right for her, Zac," she'd warned him. "They're like cream and lemon juice."

"Then who is right?" he'd demanded in exasperation. "She keeps bugging me. I had to come up with someone for her to go out with."

On Tuesday Miss P. had interrupted a counseling session to inform Zac that his matchmaking services were no longer required. Thankfully, Abby had not said *I told you so* after she'd soothed the senior's feelings. Zac didn't get how he could counsel others successfully but was unable to help this woman.

"What's the issue?" he'd demanded.

"You're trying to get her to make do, Zac," Abby had gently replied. "But the heart wants what the heart wants."

Zac's heart wanted Abby. His strong feelings took him by surprise. He longed for the right to stare into her beautiful eyes as long as possible.

To touch her velvet skin and soothe the marks she bore because of her husband's carelessness. He wanted the right to hold her, to kiss her, to spend however much time they had laughing and sharing and serving God.

So what about God?

Abby had been right all along. Zac finally faced the truth. He had no right to ask God to explain Himself.

You call him Lord, he chided his foolish pride. *But is He truly in charge of your life?*

Then it was as if a video played in his head as his brain took him through everything that had happened—the sharp sound of shots firing, witnessing his coworkers go down, blood spattering everywhere. The sudden and sickening awareness that his mission was being attacked by rebels. Terrifying thoughts of his girls being hurt by these madmen.

His final memory, the explosion of the clinic in front of him, was as unexpected, as vivid and shocking as it had been that day. He could feel the gust of heat singe his hair and toss him backward. He gasped at the memory of excruciating pain as a thousand stab wounds hit his eyes and burned so deep. He felt the solid crack against his skull. And then, mercifully, the picture went black, just as it had that day.

Zac sat, gasping for breath as he stared around

the meadow, reassuring himself that he was fine, that nothing had changed. His brain played a new sound that made his heart clench with joy. *Daddy! Daddy!* The blessed knowledge that the twins hadn't witnessed the horror. They wouldn't have the memory scars of that brutal attack to live with.

Other events rolled through his head like film from a movie. Hilarious laughter as he, Abby and the twins had tried to fly kites on probably the windiest day of the year. Joyful sounds of sharing fun in this very place. Special moments, like when he'd first seen Abby's face and how her beauty had floored him. Her touch soothing his headaches away. Her quiet calming voice, so confident of God's love, chiding him for doubting.

And the truth of God's sturdy, unyielding, overwhelming love. For him.

"I apologize," he whispered as he soaked in the enormity of it. "I demanded answers like a selfish child. I blamed You. I railed against You. Yet in spite of my tantrums, You still stuck by us."

Zac suddenly knew that he shouldn't have asked, *Why did You let it happen to me?* He should have been praising God for saving him, for sending him a friend who'd once promised he'd give his life to save Zac's daughters, and probably had. He should have been on his knees thanking God the twins were with sweet Abby. He should have been grateful for healing and love and all the other blessings he'd found at Hanging Hearts, blessings that now flowed through his life.

Including a new ministry?

Including a new love?

For a moment uncertainty welled. How did he know if either would work out? How could he face the uncertainty of a new career? Of a new love?

"With You," he said, finally yielding to the pain and loss and unanswered questions. "You will show me the way. I know that now." Head bowed, he spread his arms. "I am Your servant."

Peace flowed through him like a river until at last his soul was at rest. He leaned back and absorbed it until he felt refreshed, renewed and invigorated.

Just one question remained.

"Lord, how do I convince Abby I really care for her, that I'm not just taking the most expedient route by asking her to stay?"

Zac's phone rang. Miss P. He grimaced, then answered.

"Zac, I have some bad news."

Abby? The twins? His heart shivered. *Lord?*

"It's about that gift certificate you won for your dart skills at our family night," she said, sounding short of breath. "The place has closed and I don't know for how long."

"It doesn't ma—" True to form, she didn't let him finish.

"I am calling to invite you to dinner at my home tomorrow night. My way of making up for the mistake," she said. "Be there about six. And bring the twins. We'll have a great time together. Okay? See you then."

Without waiting for a response, she hung up.

Zac groaned aloud. No doubt she'd renew her insistence that he find her someone special. The task seemed overwhelming.

I can do all things through Christ who strengthens me. Philippians 4:13

He chuckled at the solid tug of assurance that filled him, growing his confidence. "You sure do bring those verses to mind, Father. Okay, then." He paused. "I get it. You're in charge. That's the way it's going to stay. So could You show me a way to propose to Abby? I've only got a couple more days before she leaves."

He decided to hustle back to the little log house. Maybe he could talk to her tonight, bring the subject around to feelings, specifically his for her. But on his return, Zac found his dad sitting in the living room.

"Abby asked me to take over," Ben said. "She and Bonnie are trying to finish their quilt before she leaves."

"Thanks, Dad."

So tonight was out. Maybe tomorrow? Before or after Miss P.'s dinner?

Zac sat late into the night, searching his Bible for some hint about God's plan. What he found was his own writing beside a verse. It was dated the day his mission had been attacked.

Deuteronomy 31:6—Be strong and of good courage, do not fear nor be afraid of them; for the LORD your God, He is the One who goes with you. He will not leave you nor forsake you.

"Thank you for the promise, God. Sorry I didn't understand sooner. My future is in your hands, right where it should be."

Zac wondered if God was saying, "About time!"

He fell asleep wondering how his Lord would bring him and Abby together.

Chapter Thirteen

Abby knocked on the front door and waited, admiring the gorgeous display of flowers Miss Partridge grew in her front garden.

"Did you forget your keys—" Zac stood in the doorway, staring at her.

"Hi. What are you doing here?" she asked, wondering if she'd mistaken the time or date, yet knowing she hadn't.

"The girls and I were invited for dinner. You, too?" When Abby nodded, Zac grinned. "Apparently the lady forgot to buy cream, which she insists she must have for her special mashed potatoes. She took the twins with her to get it."

Awkward was Abby's first thought.

"I thought Miss Partridge had invited me to a friendship dinner," she said, struggling to puzzle it out. "For the two of us. Maybe I got the day wrong."

"Well, come in." He swung the door wide. "I'm

sure she'll be back momentarily." He glanced at his watch and frowned.

"What?" How well she could read Zac's expressions.

"She left over twenty minutes ago. Sunshine isn't that big a town," he said as he closed the wooden door behind her. "I wonder if she's had trouble?"

"Always the negative thought first," Abby teased. She shook her head. "Miss P. never goes anywhere without her phone. If she ran into trouble she would text. Or call. She'll be here soon."

But when another twenty minutes passed and there was still no sign of her friend, Abby ran out of small talk. It was so hard to be alone with Zac, probably for the last time, and not wish things were different.

At that moment, both their phones chimed with a text.

Abby read hers, frowned, then looked at Zac. "What does yours say?"

"'My dears,'" he read aloud slowly. "'Please forgive me for my little ruse. The twins are fine with me and we shall have some fun times before I take them home and put them to bed.'" He looked up. "Yours?"

"It says the same thing. What does it mean—wait!" she exclaimed as the phones chimed a second time.

"You read this time," Zac ordered, his voice tight.

"'Dinner is ready in the oven. The table is set. Please relax and enjoy this time with each other. Blessings on you both.'" She looked up warily. "It sounds like a setup."

"Because it is. She's getting back at me for that bad match with Arthur," he exclaimed.

"By inviting me?" Abby didn't believe that, but she didn't have time to think about it.

"I'm starving," Zac insisted. "We might as well eat what she's prepared, don't you think?" He waited for her nod before ushering her to the table in the dining room, which was set with fine china, glittering crystal glassware and sparkling silver. "Nice. Wait here. I'll serve."

"No, we should do it together." She followed him into the kitchen, nose twitching at the delightful aromas wafting from there. "Smells fantastic, doesn't it?"

"Yes." He licked his lips as he lifted the dishes from the oven. "I hope she made that chocolate cake for dessert."

Abby pulled a sticky note off the fridge.

"Salad," she said as she reached in to retrieve it and the dressing for it. "So fresh and inviting."

"You can have all of it. I'd rather eat this." He held out a glass-covered dish with browned cutlets in it.

"You don't even know what it is," Abby teased.

"Yes, I do. Veal cutlets. She asked me earlier this week if they were still my preference. I had no idea why." He carried it and the other side dishes to the table.

"She's seated us close together so we don't have to reach, I guess," Abby said as she sat in the chair he held for her.

Zac sat down next to her, his arm brushing hers. "Cozy," was all he said before he gave thanks.

Abby started with her salad, her heart thumping merrily each time Zac got close. She wanted to savor every moment of this evening so she could take it out and remember the details when she was far away and all alone.

"How did the session today go?" she asked.

"Not great." He set his half-full salad bowl aside and leaned back to wait for her. "I was too distracted."

There was something different about him, something…relaxed? She gave up on the salad.

"Distracted by?"

"My stupidity." He served her creamy mashed potatoes with a faint aroma of garlic, glazed carrots, fresh peas and, of course, the veal.

"What are you talking about, Zac?" Had something happened? What had she missed? Abby suddenly regretted her decision to take the twins for a long hike this afternoon. She should have been there...

"Stop worrying," he said, covering her hand with his. "It's nothing bad. I just had a reality check. Enjoy your meal before it gets cold," he urged, but she noticed his other hand shook slightly as he tore apart a freshly baked roll.

Nervous? Why would Zac be uncomfortable with her?

Abby tasted the food, allowing the delicious flavors to mingle on her tongue. But she couldn't sidetrack her thoughts from what he'd said.

"What kind of reality check?" she wondered when she couldn't control her curiosity a moment longer.

"Oh, God and I had a little set-to." It sounded like he was toying with her, until Abby saw the way his eyes glinted when he tipped his head to the side and allowed her a closer look.

"Zac?" she whispered uneasily. "What's really going on?"

"With Miss P.? I haven't a clue. With me?" He took off his glasses and set them aside. "I finally admitted to myself that God loves me and that I love you."

"Pardon?" She was afraid to believe it, afraid she'd only heard what she wanted to. Her heart trembled when he pushed away their dishes and grasped her hands.

"I said I love you. I know I haven't acted like it. I've been running scared, Abby."

She heard the tremor in his voice. "Scared of me?" she whispered.

"Of you. Of God. Of life." A small mocking smile lifted his lips. "It's a very uncomfortable position. Which is probably why I've been such a bear these past few months…" He stopped abruptly when her forefinger pressed against his lips to stop him.

"You had some things to figure out. Please tell me."

"I was in Peace Meadow," he said, shaking his head. "There's something about that place since you fixed it up…"

"We relax there. We relinquish our barriers," she murmured, thinking of her own faith renewal that had taken place there. "Then God can open our eyes and show us how foolish we're being."

"Foolish is the right term," he said, his fingers tightening on hers. "I finally saw that I am the child and He is the parent."

"And the mission?" she wondered, peering at his beloved face and soaking in every detail, praying this wasn't a dream she'd wake up from.

"May I tell you about *that* day?" His brown eyes turned to cocoa while his face tightened into a mask. "I feel like if I tell you, if I share the worst day of my life with you, it will somehow cleanse the horrible memories."

"Then tell me," Abby invited, thrilled he'd decided to share these most personal details with her.

So Zac bared his soul, bringing light to every dark detail, every horrifying image and every lingering fear that still lurked in the corners of his mind.

"I'm so sorry you had to go through that," she said when he'd finished. She cupped his jaw in her palm. "I'm so, so sorry." She blinked when he turned his lips and placed a kiss in the center of her hand.

"Thank you, darling heart. But I'm not." He grinned at her surprise. "Oh, I'd like to have my full sight back, don't get me wrong. But I think God had to take me into the realm of the sightless in order to get me to see that pain and suffering aren't a waste. To teach me more about Him, force me to learn what I didn't want to."

"And what did you learn?" she whispered, half-afraid to hear the answer. But why fear? Wasn't God in charge?

"I learned that my ways are not His ways. Obvious, huh?" Zac's fingers began toying with her hair, coiling it about his fingers. "I realized that you are a beautiful, giving person, inside and out, and that you somehow learned to reach past your pain to help others. I learned humility. Truly I did," he said when she smiled. Then his voice dropped, grew serious. "I learned something else."

She hardly dared hope...

"I also learned I love you, Abigail Armstrong. I've been desperately praying you might possibly feel something for me, that my anger and harshness and bitter tirade haven't hurt you."

"Oh, Zac." Abby touched her lips to his chin. "I'm so proud of you. You've worked your way through a very hard, costly time and you've come out shining on the other side. Your new ministry is a true gift from God and you use it to glorify Him. You love God, don't you?"

"Yes, I do." He nodded, his gaze never leaving her face. "I have been blessed with two earthly fathers who both taught me that my being, who I am, comes from my heavenly Father. I think I forgot that for a while."

"I'm so glad you've remembered." She smiled at him, somehow shy.

"But you haven't answered me." He frowned. "Does that mean you don't have any feelings for me, Abby? Did I spoil everything by being so self-centered?"

"No." She moistened her lips, half-afraid to say it, yet determined not to let this God-given opportunity pass her by. "I love you, Zac. I have for some time. Oh!"

She gulped as he grasped her hand and eased her from the table right into his arms.

"Seriously? You love me?" he demanded, staring into her face.

"Well, of course—"

The rest of her words were stifled by his kiss, tender and loving, yet strong, showing her without a doubt that she was the woman of his heart. And Abby responded, tentatively at first, and then, throwing worry to the wind, with her entire being.

And when the storm had passed and they stood embracing each other beside the perfectly set table still bearing the sumptuous but cooling meal, Abby giggled.

"What's so funny?" Zac demanded.

"We're standing in Miss Partridge's dining room, kissing. Imagine if she saw us?"

But Zac only laughed and shook his head.

"I kind of think that was her whole aim in inviting us both here tonight," he said. "She decided to play matchmaker to the matchmakers, and truthfully, I think she's much better at it than us."

Abby agreed as she gave silent thanks to God for granting her heart's dearest wish—to love and be loved.

"The only thing is, I have nothing but love to offer you, my darling. Not a paying job or a place to call my own." Zac brushed tiny kisses against the scar on her neck. "I don't even know where all this counseling will lead."

"None of us know what tomorrow holds," she said, reveling in his embrace. "It's called living by faith."

"Yes. So will you marry me and live by faith with me?" he asked. "I don't see very well, I'm stubborn and opinionated and—"

"And the most wonderful man God could have chosen for me," she finished happily. "Yes and yes. When?"

"As soon as we can arrange it." He kissed her once more to seal their pledge and then made a face.

"What's that for?" she asked, enjoying the touch of his face under her fingertips.

"The twins already announced our faux engagement," he reminded her. "This is going to be rather anticlimactic news for everyone else."

"That won't stop Mia and Zoe from telling it, though." Abby laughed. "Not that they'll need any help. Miss P. has probably already beaten them to it." She fell into thought, the laughter dying.

"What's wrong?" Zac nudged her chin up with

his knuckle. "What are you worrying about, be-loved?"

"I'm not sure I'll make a very good mis-sionary's wife," she murmured. "Not like your Maria."

"Maria wasn't perfect, Abby," Zac said. "You have the most beautiful eyes." He blinked when she tapped his cheek. "Sorry, I got distracted."

She laughed at that.

"Anyway, listen, darling. Maria had faults. She burned every meal she cooked for the first two years of our marriage. She was a lot smarter than me when it came to diagnosing and parenting, and she constantly reminded me of that fact. So what? I loved her, anyway. But she's gone and you're here and I love you. Is Maria going to be a problem for you?"

"I don't know," Abby answered truthfully. "I wasn't a very good wife to Ken. What if I make mistakes?"

"What if I do? Will you forgive me?"

"Of course. I love you." She punctuated that with a kiss.

"And I love you. I loved Maria, Abby, but she's my past, just as Ken is yours." He smiled that dear beloved smile that promised the world. "We are different people now. You are my future. I want us to work, play and grow old together. I want us to teach the twins about God. I want to help anyone who seeks me out, if I can." He drew back to give emphasis to his next words. "But it's only doable if you're there with me, encouraging, helping, reminding and teaching me about my priorities."

"Not even your horses on the Double H could drag me away now," she whispered before she leaned in for his kiss.

Abby loved the way Zac held her, as if she were the most precious thing in his world. For the rest of her life she would remember this evening and the love Miss Partridge had helped them both realize.

"What?" she murmured when he eventually drew away.

"I was just wondering if our matchmaker made that special chocolate cake for us." He winked at her.

"Zac! You're thinking about dessert at a moment like this?" She pretended to scold him, but in truth she wanted to share that special treat with him. She wanted to share every moment, every dream, every laugh and every tear with this man. "I think it's in the fridge," she guessed as she carried their plates to the kitchen.

"Wrong." Zac deposited the serving dishes on the counter, then pointed. "It's in that big old cabinet."

"How do you know?"

"Because when she was grilling me on anatomy all those years ago, and was finally satisfied that I knew my lessons, she'd invite me over here for a treat and she'd always, always take it out of that cabinet."

Abby opened the door and started laughing. Zac looked over her shoulder. Soon he, too, was grinning from ear to ear.

The chocolate cake was there with *Congratulations!* written across it in perfectly formed white letters.

With the flourish of a maître d' in a fancy dining room, Zac cut them each a slice. They sat together at the breakfast bar, enjoying every bite, until he put down his fork and grabbed her hand.

"My darling, we must find Miss P. a very special man. She deserves it for doing this for us." He paused, grinned. "And just think of the treats she'll give us for that."

"You know what I love most about you, Zac?" Abby said, twining her arms around his neck.

"What?" he demanded, kissing her chin.

"Everything."

Later they cleaned up the house before returning to the ranch to thank their dear friend for her part in their joy. Alone at last in the little log house, with the twins sleeping soundly, Abby pulled a notebook out of her bag and sat down next to Zac.

"Serious candidates for Miss Partridge," she said, pen at the ready.

"A boyfriend could be our wedding present to her," Zac murmured. "If we could find him in time."

"A wedding. We have to plan a wedding." Abby's brain glazed over as she began dreaming about her future.

She rubbed her shoulder against Zac and turned to a new, clean page titled *Wedding*.

Epilogue

The morning of Zac's marriage to Abby dawned bright and clear with nary a cloud in the sky. Since they were having an outdoor wedding, he thought that was a good sign. He and Drew had just finished gathering wildflowers for table decor when his phone rang.

"Good morning, wife-to-be."

"Zac, I need to talk to you. It's urgent." Abby's tone worried him.

"What's wrong?" he asked while his brain begged God to solve it, whatever it was.

"Absolutely nothing. In fact, something is marvelous. Meet me in Peace Meadow in fifteen minutes," she ordered briskly.

"But we're not supposed to see each other—"

"Seriously?" Abby demanded, her tone scathing. "You're going to cling to some blather about silly traditions when we serve the God of the universe?"

"No, dear," he answered, totally chastened. "Be there in ten."

"Henpecked already? Have I told you how much I love my new sister-in-law-to-be?" Drew's grin said it was payback time. "Fantastic woman you're marrying. Won't let you get away with anything. Can I help?"

"Just be there with me, at the right time. And don't lose that ring," Zac warned. Then he sighed. "I sure wish our brother could be here. Having Sam home would make it perfect."

"It's already perfect, bro. You're marrying the woman of your dreams. Now go do as she says."

"Yeah." Zac hurried out the door and along the path, hanging on to the rope more as a memory than necessity. In Peace Meadow he saw Abby standing by the gazebo, her hair in huge rollers and some green gunk plastered over her face. "Yeow," he said as he found a not-too-sticky spot on her cheek to kiss.

"This mask is Miss Partridge's idea. It's supposed to make me beautiful." She touched her face and grimaced. "I just hope I don't break out."

"You already are beautiful, Abby." Zac glanced around, then looked at her again. "What's up?"

"You do realize you're marrying a genius, don't you?" she demanded, her face wreathed in a grin.

"Old news to this supernerd." He dodged her playful swat. "So tell me what's happening, genius."

"I had the most incredible idea this morning while I was out walking. Do you know what's behind this gazebo?"

"Uh, trees," he guessed, unsure of what he was supposed to say. "And a creek."

"And then what?" she demanded.

"Not Hanging Hearts land," he said. What was going on?

"I know but hear me out." Abby grabbed his hand and began painting a mental picture. "What if we bought that land? We could abut Peace Meadow and build a house so we're overlooking the meadow. A big house. With plenty of bedrooms." She paused, waited for his response.

"Uh—okay." Zac stared at her, then turned to view the property.

"We'd cut down a few of the trees, just enough for access. We could build a stone bridge so you could get across." He must have looked confused because Abby began speaking faster and faster. "People could stay overnight with us if they needed more time with you. You could continue to see them in the meadow and your family could easily visit us. It would be perfect."

Zac was beginning to see her vision.

"It would be," he agreed quietly, hating that he had to dull her enthusiasm. "But that's not our land, Abby."

"No. That's true. It isn't." She grabbed his arm

and tugged him along to a little space in the trees. "Look up there. To the right?"

Zac couldn't see anything.

"It's a sign," she said with great glee. "For Sale. This could be ours, darling. We could buy it and turn it into a center where you can continue your work. It would be perfect."

"It *would* be perfect, my darling. Anywhere with you is perfect." Zac drew her into his arms. "But, sweetheart, I don't have the kind of money it would take to buy that land and build on it."

"I do." She wrapped her arms around him and laid her sticky green cheek next to his. "More than enough to build a house for us, too."

"But, Abby," he protested, drawing back. "That's your money, from your parents. You wanted to do something to honor them."

"Yes, I do. And this is it." As she glared at him flakes of her green mask began to peel off. "You're not going to give me some silly protest about the husband providing for his wife, are you? Because I won't listen. If I'm marrying you, we share. Agreed?"

"But—" Zac turned, glanced back over Peace Meadow, then up the small incline where she hoped their home would sit.

"My parents would be ecstatic to know that money was being used for a wellness center to help people learn more about God. That's exactly what they dedicated their lives to." As Abby studied him, the joy she'd glowed with moments ago slowly leeched away. "I'm sorry, Zac. I can see you don't want this. I just thought—" Her head ducked down to hide the tears he knew were gathering. "I got carried away."

"Daddy! Abby's crying." Zoe squeezed out from beneath the bench in the gazebo.

"Yeah, crying. Aren't you going to kiss her better?" Mia demanded.

"We don't want our mom to cry on the getting-married day," Zoe insisted, her forehead creased.

Zac studied them, one by one, feeling like he'd been ambushed. And then he realized that he was going to have to amp up his vision, not of his eyes but of his faith, to keep up with his wife and family.

"A wellness center, our own land, a precious wife and two nosy kids who spy on us," he said, and burst into laughter. "God is going to drown me with blessings."

The girls raced over and grabbed his legs, giggling like crazy. Abby studied him, her tears having turned the gunk on her face into green-glue rivers.

"Ours," she whispered. "Yes. Together."

"I'll go over and put down a deposit on our dream before the pastor arrives to marry us," he promised. "I can manage that."

"Is it too much?" she asked when he pulled her into his arms.

"No way. You just keep dreaming, wifey. I'll keep running to catch up to you." He kissed her thoroughly, right in front of his daughters, who watched unabashedly.

"Wifey?" She frowned.

"Seemed appropriate with that stuff on your face." He froze as a voice shrieked across Peace Meadow.

"Abigail Armstrong, you come back here right now! I'm managing this wedding and we will not have any goof-ups!" Miss Partridge warned.

"Might have been a mistake to give her that responsibility," Zac whispered for Abby's ears alone.

"Never. The more the merrier to join us on our ride through life." She tugged him forward by his shirt and planted a kiss on his lips that left him breathless. "Don't be late, hubby-to-be," she counseled. "Miss P. won't like it. Neither will I."

Hand in hand, a twin on either side, they walked toward the woman who'd become such a good friend.

"Abigail, let us get into the house, please. Zac." She nodded at him sternly.

"Miss Partridge." He stepped forward and brushed her cheek with his lips. "You are amazing. Don't even think of moving away. We need you."

"Wherever would I be moving to when I have

your single brother to counsel once I get this wedding under way?" She shook her head at him, then shooed the twins toward his log house.

"Sam's here?" Zac couldn't stop grinning. "My long-lost brother returns on the day I get to marry the most beautiful woman in the world and plan our next venture. So fitting."

"Yes, it is," Miss Partridge said primly. "And he has a friend with him. John somebody who wants to see you." She grabbed Abby's hand to pull her forward but Zac wouldn't let go.

"John," he said, staring into her eyes. "Could it be—what else do you suppose God has planned for us?"

Her beautiful smile radiated joy as her fingers grazed over his face and across his lips.

"Just have to wait and see, Mr. Missionary," she said with a smile.

Zac nodded, his heart singing. "As long as you're right beside me, Mrs. Missionary."

"Abigail!" Miss Partridge called. "Do hurry, dear. We don't have all day."

Abby looked at Zac. They both burst into laughter before racing toward their matchmaker and the future God had planned for them at Hanging Hearts Ranch.

* * * * *

*If you enjoyed this story, pick up these
other stories from Lois Richer:*

A Dad for Her Twins
Rancher Daddy
Gift-Wrapped Family
Accidental Dad
Meant-to-Be Baby
Mistletoe Twins
Rocky Mountain Daddy
Rocky Mountain Memories
Hoping for a Father

*Available now from Love Inspired!
Find more great reads at
www.LoveInspired.com.*

Dear Reader,

Welcome back to Hanging Hearts Ranch. It's always nice to come home, though perhaps not under Zac's circumstances. It took time for him to understand that losing his mission and being blinded was only another step along the path to serving God. Abby, too, experienced deep loss, first her child and her husband, then the orphanage where she soothed her aching heart by ministering to needy kids. But God had so much more planned for both their futures.

Perhaps that's a lesson we all need to learn. God doesn't make mistakes. There's a reason for the bumps and stumbles we experience, though we may not understand why at the time.

I hope you'll join me again soon for Sam Calhoun's story. Meantime, I'd love to hear from you, either through this publisher, via email at loisricher@gmail.com, at my website loisricher.com or on Facebook.

Till we meet again, may you truly experience the joy of knowing God our Father is with you all the time, in every situation.

Blessings,

Lois Richer